Aya Dunbar is a Palestinian author, born and raised in Jerusalem. She holds a bachelor's degree in Human Rights and International Law and a minor in Literature and Society. Aya has a passion for writing. She spends most of her free time writing and turning feelings and ideas into stories. She started writing short paragraphs until she found herself with full chapters, and in the end, her chapters became a novel. She believes that all thoughts should be ink on paper so that the world does not miss out on the adventures of the mind.

To all the women out there who are still trapped in an abusive relationship. To those who have tried to escape ninety-nine times, thinking that there was no way out. The attempt number one hundred will be the final time.

Breaking out of the shadows forms the shining light that has long waited for your power.

Aya Dunbar

Smitten: Beneath the Layers of the Holy Land

AUSTIN MACAULEY PUBLISHERS™

LONDON • CAMBRIDGE • NEW YORK • SHARJAH

Ordering Information
Quantity sales: Special discounts are available on quantity purchases by corporations, associations, and others. For details, contact the publisher at the address below.

Publisher's Cataloging-in-Publication data
Dunbar, Aya
Smitten: Beneath the Layers of the Holy Land

ISBN 9798891556416 (Paperback)
ISBN 9798891556423 (Hardback)
ISBN 9798891556430 (ePub e-book)

Library of Congress Control Number: 2024913546

www.austinmacauley.com/us

First Published 2024
Austin Macauley Publishers LLC
40 Wall Street, 33rd Floor, Suite 3302
New York, NY 10005
USA

mail-usa@austinmacauley.com
+1 (646) 5125767

If I were to start naming the people who helped me bring this work to life, I would fill countless pages.

When I finished the last chapters, I was overwhelmed and happy at the same time. Given that this is my first novel, I felt lost and wondered what comes next. Mrs. Gwendolyn Socol Rosenbluth read my first draft and did the proofreading. Mrs. Socol Rosenbluth corrected my mistakes by hand and left me a heartwarming letter. We never met in person, but she was willing to help a stranger. I will be forever grateful for her help.

I would also like to thank Mr. Samer Nammari. Mr. Nammari was a great help when the manuscript was still in progress. He revised some chapters and gave helpful feedback.

To my friends and especially my favorite person Lara for putting up with my emotional outbursts.

To my family, who always had my back.

I would like to thank the people who have caused me pain. It was only through these moments of pain that I was able to write something.

I would like to thank the moments of happiness that also inspired me to write imaginary stories.

I thank my feelings and my overthinking. I have always been criticized for having 'too much' emotions, and I have been called an overthinker. Having 'too much' emotions has helped me pour my feelings on paper and turn them into a work of art.

Table of Contents

Write	11
The Forbidden Fruit Dare to Touch It	12
Year After Year Our Honeymoon	13
The Glimpse of Heaven Before Entering Hell	18
The Drunk Groom	21
Victorious Night	25
The Triangle and the Square	31
Salma a Vampire Sucking Money Out of Men	35
Hide and Seek	40
Neglected	43
The Snail and Its Shell	46
Cold Affection	48
Dirty Bed Sheets	50
The Souvenir	56
Revenge?	63
A Shoulder to Lean On	68
My Cursed Fetus	69
Tahseen	75
The Miracle of Birth April 2018	78
Motherhood	83

A Mistake That Led to Our Existence   88

Smashed   90

Pestiferous Reality   97

The Guy I Used to Know   103

Slaughtering What Was Left of Us   106

Al-Istikhaara Prayer   110

Her Shadow Erasing or Rewriting Every Line in Our Story   113

The Crucial Dreams   121

Next Deadly Dream   124

Gluing Broken Pieces or Ending a Disaster   125

The Harvey Specter of Jerusalem, October 2018   129

Love Vs. Hate   136

The Fool and the Charming Husband ~Part 1~   137

The Fool and the Charming Husband ~Part 2~   144

The Fool and the Charming Husband ~Part 3~   147

The Provocative Wedding   151

The Fool and the Charming Husband ~Part 4~   153

The Mighty Elders   158

Feminism?   161

Fusty Thinking   163

Saif the Trainee   164

The Old City of Jerusalem   166

Massive Destruction   169

A Clean Chapter   172

As Sweet As Kunafeh Saif   174

Write

Write until your hands betray you and fall apart.
Write for each illiterate one, even if they won't read your words.
Write for your bygone or current lover.
Learn to value new words.
Don't let your thoughts fade away before you put them on paper.
Document the events lived in your imagination.
Don't forget the stories that were tailored in your head.
Remember the love scenes that were lived by you and the ghosts inside your head.
Feel the heartbreaks, the tears, and the harming kisses.
If you can't have great memories in your life, then never forget that you can create ones in your far-away imaginary space.
You exist everywhere.
You are here in person and you are somewhere else in spirit.

The Forbidden Fruit
Dare to Touch It

The idea of this story resembles a forbidden fruit that is presented as a sacred gift for society. It exists, but we're not allowed to replace it, speak its name, or even rebel against it. We're forced to accept it and the consequences it brings in our lives because no one believes your word against it.

Everyone thinks that it brings good nutrition to society, while it's just rotten and contagious. No one dares to fight it, and by no one, I mean the weak and soundless people.

The forbidden fruit represents the men in power who rule over our lives and think that they know what's best for us. Their shield is too shiny and allows them to hide the true viciousness that lies beneath their skin that lies beneath their surface. They fight our battles for their own benefit. Breaking us helps them climb that ladder toward a stronger rule over the people and build a reputation out of it.

The forbidden fruit smashes anyone that comes its way and whoever thinks of fighting back against its system.

Year After Year
Our Honeymoon

Have you ever felt the same feeling you had a year ago?

In February 2019, I was able to relive and remember what happened to me in February 2017. Every year, season, and month I recall what happened to me in previous days, months, and years.

Today, I was able to relive the memories of my honeymoon. I remember that we spent half a day sightseeing in France together. We were too exhausted to finish our tour so we decided to finish our meal and head back to the hotel for a break. We both agreed to go to a night club at midnight. He wanted me to explore the night life since I had never been to a club before. After all, everything is possible and allowed on honeymoons. What is considered taboo becomes acceptable to do and experience the foreign land. No one knew him in France; therefore, his reputation wouldn't be ruined by his wife's behavior. No one would know what happened, and he would act as if it had never occurred when we returned home.

We both reclined on our fancy bed, facing our breathtaking sea-view window. I had paid for all the hotel expenses by choice. He couldn't afford a honeymoon on his own, he said. I was too dreamy and had to get a honeymoon anywhere outside of our miserable and conflicted country. In return, he was generous enough to pay for the food at the luxurious restaurants. He refused to use public transportation. We chose taxies as our only way to commute from one place to another. "Our honeymoon shouldn't be like any other normal day," he would say. I felt that he wanted to pay me back since I had taken care of the hotel and our flight. In return, he paid for everything else. I thought that we would spend our lives sharing everything together. I had hoped that this would be the case with his feelings as well. I had hoped for a fifty-fifty relationship, but I paid more in feelings than he did.

We both agreed to get some rest and sleep before our glorious night—the night that he would take the lead and be my guide through the world of sins.

He grabbed me closer to him and started kissing me on the lips. I had always been aroused by his lips, and most of all by his hands. His hands had always smelled like cigarettes. The trace of cigarettes between his fingers was my strange attraction. I've never imagined that this smell would be my favorite scent.

He didn't try to fuck me this time. He was tired and gave up trying. He had been trying to steal away my virginity ever since our wedding night, barely with any luck to achieve the task. Whenever he would try to put his penis between my thighs to reach my intimate parts, I would close my legs as hard as I could and push him away with my hands. I was terrified. All the myths that I had heard during my childhood about accidentally losing my virginity made me overprotective of my hymen. I've been told to keep my legs closed and not let anyone touch my forbidden spot all my life.

I closed my eyes trying not to think about anything other than the feeling of his arms wrapped around me.

I snapped out of my sleep to realize that we had overslept and that it was 11:30 p.m. I had been planning to wake up earlier to get dressed for my big night. I called his name three times in a row while shaking his shoulder with my shivering hand. I wasn't fully awake, but the monster that arose from his body helped open my eyes to my upcoming reality. He jumped out of bed, screaming and cursing God's existence. He started moving around the room with his hands on his head while mouthing poisoning words, "Oh, you damn God! Fuck God! She shakes my fucking body as if a war is about to begin! Oh, you filthy God!"

He moved toward me quickly after he finished his run around the room yelling directly at my face, "Is this how you awaken a human being? Adi! Adi! Fuck God! Oh, may God be cursed!" Then he shifted unconsciously toward the TV that was placed on a wooden table with a glass top. His next angry move was hammering the glass top with both hands and ended up smashing it. This action made me unfreeze and run to the bathroom to lock myself in.

I sat in the corner of the bathroom on the cold ground. I wrapped my arms around my knees, shaking with tears crawling down my face. I started thinking about ending my marriage before it even started. I thought about divorce but feared the idea of getting accused of being the reason behind this failure. *What shall I tell everyone when I get back home? I will be a divorced virgin if I take this step. Will people even believe that I am a virgin? Will he accuse me of having a pre-marital affair that had led to this divorce? Will they say that her husband found out that she was not a virgin and divorced her after a couple of days?* I had different scenarios in my head as to what would happen if I ended my marriage with this savage animal. After all, my society was based on rumors and since girls are always the vulnerable characters in the stories, they would blame me for what had happened in mine.

The echo of the room became speechless. His voice was turned on mute. I took this as a sign there was an end to the massacre that had just taken place outside. I stepped outside the bathroom with fear and anger in my throat. He didn't look me in the eye. He had his hands tied to his head staring at the wooden floor. I slowly walked back to bed in baby steps. I sat on the bed with the sheets covering my legs and with my back against the headboard of the bed.

He left the room and when he returned, he told me to cover my breasts with my robe. A cleaning lady came in to observe the shattered glass situation. She called someone using a communication device. I couldn't understand what she was saying since I had limited knowledge of French. A man followed in based on her request. He glared at me with irritation searching for evidence of bruises on my body or face. He shifted toward my beloved maniac to ask him about the incident. "How was it broken?"

Adi started acting with his body on the fake events of the incident. "I slipped and accidentally broke it since both of my elbows had their weight on the glass."

Disbelief was drawn all over the stranger's face. "No," he replied in English and moved toward the table to reenact what had actually happened. He raised both of his hands and acted as if he was slamming the table. He gazed back at Adi with mockery and told him that he'd take care of the mess.

I stared at my husband while he was asleep and wanted to choke him till he died. I didn't kill him, but a part of me was murdered when I slept with tears covering the white pillow underneath my head. I was a bride covered in white while on the inside I was dressed as a widow in black. I never thought that my white wedding dress was going to be my shroud.

I got up the next day trying to overcome the anger that I had in my chest. I took a shower, put makeup on, dressed in one of my honeymoon dresses, and went to grab my bag to go outside. He was staring at me all the while trying to understand what I was doing and how I was about to ignore what had happened the previous night.

"Where are you going?" He dared to ask.

"I am going out to explore the city," I replied without looking at him.

He held my hand trying to stop me from leaving him alone.

"Please leave my hand. I came here to have fun. I won't waste my time with you here," I demanded.

He dragged me to sit on the bed while he sat on the ground in front of me. "I beg you to forgive me! I told you before about my anger issues and that I need time to function after I wake up. You frightened me when you called my name several times—I am really sorry! Please wait for me to get dressed and we'll go out together."

I started crying, ruining the makeup that I had spent fifteen minutes putting on. "I don't want to speak to you right now. Just let me go and we'll talk after I return," I sobbed.

"Where will you go?" He simply asked.

"I want to go shopping and explore the city. Please leave me alone. I cannot even look at you." I snapped out of the bed trying to escape his grasp.

"Habibti, I am really sorry. I will make it up to you, I swear. Fuck me for ruining your night! Please forgive me." He cursed himself as a way to win my sympathy.

"Leave me the hell alone! I don't want to spend the day with you. I am not even sure I want to spend my life with you anymore," I shrugged.

"You're saying this because you're angry at me. You don't mean it. I know you love me. Saba, I cannot imagine my life without you. Please let me make it up to you." He breathed heavily as he wiped mascara-mixed tears off of my face with a napkin and then shifted to kiss my hands. "I am really sorry; I will never do that again." He made his promises and moved on to joke about the scars that he had on his hands. "I slept with my hands open so you would feel sorry for me because of the cuts that are on my hands. I was bleeding and you didn't care."

"You deserve it," I replied with satisfaction.

I did wait for him and fixed my makeup. I felt sorry for him even though I should've felt sorry for myself for what I had seen the night before. I was too much in love to hold a grudge. On that day, he kept me closer to him; he kept on hugging and kissing me the whole day. Whenever I was mean to him or said something that would have made him angry, he would ignore it and obey my demands. He spoiled me like a child who craved attention.

The Glimpse of Heaven Before Entering Hell

The calm before the storm—this famous Arabic saying resembled the phase of my engagement before I became married. Adi had always mentioned that he had anger issues. Everyone who saw us together would start joking about it and would warn me of the anger problem that Adi had, and in such times, I would provoke him by saying, *I want to start a fight with you just to see what this fuss is all about.* I wanted to explore his angry side before I got trapped in the same house with him. He would laugh at my wish and say that he could not imagine a day where he would get angry at me or even harm me. "When I am around you, I am different, and you make me feel relaxed. Your calmness is affecting my behavior."

I remember the day we drove all the way to Ramallah to have dinner. On that day, the sound of rain hammering on the car's window was our companion. It was freezing outside, but luckily warm inside the restaurant. Adi started the night with one glass of whiskey with two cubes of ice only. No more than two and no less than two. He beckoned the waitress to take our order. At the end of our dinner, he closed the night with two glasses of whiskey only, no more and no less than two.

"I won't let you drive. I'll be your chauffeur for the night, my love," I declared.

We left the restaurant with Adi's hands wrapped around my waist.

I was about to start the engine when Adi's hand reached mine to stop me. "Stop. It's still raining, and no one can see through the windows with all the fog."

"My dad will kill me if I get home late, and it's already eleven. Let's wrap up the night with a passionate kiss," I offered, to try to compensate for my need to get home.

"We'll wrap up the night as it should be wrapped. Don't worry about your dad; he's probably asleep now," he assured me.

I wanted to keep on protesting and maybe stop him. Instead, I let him slide my car seat to the back so he would get on top of me. I surrendered after he slid his hand down to my intimate area while printing his lips all over my neck.

I kissed him gently on the forehead telling him that we should start moving.

"I can't wait to share a house with you and stop sneaking around to steal a kiss or hide to be able to do what we did," he whispered after he got back to his seat with his head jerked back. As a response, I leaned over to him and kissed him on the lips while mouthing, "Soon, my love."

When we were engaged, I never dared to let him carry out the act to a conclusion. We were satisfied with foreplay—I couldn't afford to lose my virginity before my wedding day.

I fixed my clothes and what was ruined of my makeup with the wet wipes that were in my purse and headed home.

Adi was moving his body from left to right listening to old Arabic music that was aired on the radio. I kept turning my head toward him with a big smile on my face enjoying seeing him relaxed and happy. The feeling of love was floating in my head and swimming its way through my body.

My thoughts were interrupted by the voice of Adi yelling, "Stop the car now."

He asked me to stop the vehicle but his body couldn't stop dancing.

I did as requested and stopped on the side of the highway. I watched him jump out of the car, screaming my name as he continued dancing on the side of the street. I couldn't help but enjoy the movie scene he was acting out. I laughed so hard that night until my mouth started hurting. "Come on, my dear Saba. Join me!"

Instead of joining him, I started recording his solo party to keep this memory alive.

As a closure for the night, I got scolded by my parents for getting home at 2:00 a.m. I was allowed to go to bed after I promised my father that this action would not happen ever again until I got married.

I placed my head on my pillow and turned my phone to text my beloved Adi.

"Let me know when you get home Habibi." 2:24

"I am home. How did it go with your father?" 2:25

"I had a rough lecture, but this night was worth it." 2:26

"I can't wait to close my eyes with your body next to mine in the same bed." 2:28

"Me too! <3 I love you, Adi." 2:28

"You're my soul Saba. I love you too." 2:29

The Drunk Groom

I had always scrolled videos on Facebook showing grooms' reactions when they set eyes on their brides for the first time at weddings. My heart would melt whenever I would see the sparkle of love each couple had in their eyes. The universe vanished around them, and they only saw each other. I never thought that I would care that much about Adi's reaction when he saw me for the first time in my snowy, white dress.

The day began when he promised that he would pick me up from the hair salon at noon. "Don't be late or I will kill you, Adi Makhlouf. I will ruin your day! I'll be waiting for you at 12:00 p.m. my dear future husband."

He flushed my words down the toilet on that day. I texted him our usual good morning text but didn't get a response. I didn't panic and pushed aside the idea of him being asleep, even though all the signs were pointing toward my deepest fear of getting disappointed by his neglectful act.

The hairdresser finished with my hair and makeup at the exact time that I had in mind, but my future husband didn't keep his promise. I called him ten times while my sister was helping me slide into my dress. She kept on assuring me that he'd make it on time. I waited for 15 minutes before the salon door was opened to reveal the presence of his two sisters. Salma had her hand on her mouth while mumbling, "Oh, my God! You look stunning. Wow, just wow!"

"Really? You think so?" I asked.

Tala replied to affirm what Salma had said. I moved on with my second question. "Where is he? He's asleep, isn't he?"

Salma's voice shook while she answered me, saying, "No. He woke up an hour ago. Hopefully, he'll be here soon. Don't worry, dear."

The hairdresser jumped in to comfort me. "It happens with all brides. I never had a groom who came on time for his bride."

Their words stopped being comforting when the first hour passed by. I called him five more times till he finally answered. "You're an hour late, Adi. A full hour! Where the hell are you?"

He muttered in a calm and relaxing voice, "I am at the barbershop, sweetie. I will be done soon."

"Soon? Define soon. Explain it by giving me a time. Ten minutes soon? Or an hour soon? Adi, you promised!" I tried to remain calm even though my sentences were screaming out on my behalf.

"I am so sorry, Habibti. I stayed up all night yesterday celebrating with my friends," he calmly replied.

"What about my celebration? You're starting to ruin my day. We still have to take our wedding photos." I was choking with disappointment.

"Can't we skip this part? You know I hate being photographed. I love being behind the camera, not in front of it." He tried to escape the first ritual that would document our day.

"Adi, it's our wedding day. I want to capture our big day. I want this memory to be saved," I had to state the obvious.

We finished the phone call with a promise that he'll be there for me soon. Unfortunately, two more hours passed leaving me frozen on a chair that was in the middle of the salon in my big fluffy wedding gown.

My nerves waged a war against my mind until I heard Tala calling, "He's here. He's parking the car." I stood up waiting for him while Tala fixed my dress from behind. He entered the salon all groomed. Everyone at the salon paused awaiting his reaction, observing the two of us to witness our special moment.

"Are you ready to go?" He asked. This is what he had to say when he saw me. I was able to sense that the hair stylist felt pity for me. I swallowed my soreness and affirmed that I was ready. He paid the hairdresser and we headed out. My sister and my unworthy groom helped me get into the car.

"You didn't comment on the way I look. Don't I look gorgeous?" I was forced to ask.

He looked at me through the mirror that was centered before his eyes in the car and expressed how lovely I looked. "You look marvelous, my love. I expected you to look amazing, and you're truly more astonishing than I had imagined."

"Don't lie to me. Tell me what you really think." His first disappointing reaction made me question his answer.

"I swear on my mother's honor that this is the truth. The prettiest bride I have ever seen." He honey-buttered his answer.

His coldness provoked me and made me determined to ruin the rest of our day since he had already ruined the first part of it. "Now that we're over with this, it's time to scold you for being late. You left me there for more than two hours and you promised not to!"

He tried to pull my sister into this by asking her to help him calm me down. I ignored what he asked my sister for and kept on polluting the atmosphere of the car with my disappointment. "You ruined my day, Adi."

He tried to calm me down and failed. In return, he got furious as well. "Everyone is expecting to see us soon. We cannot stay like this."

"You care about people's opinions, but you don't care about how you made me feel?" I yelled with frustration.

A big fight was about to start when we noticed that a group of tourists were taking pictures of us and waving at us. The situation forced us to wave back and laugh. They showed up just in time to flip our mood. My sister sighed. "I wish they had showed up earlier to calm the storm we had earlier."

After the first hour of our wedding party, the groom disappeared from the 'women-only' hall. Adi didn't agree to a mixed wedding since his family was somehow conservative, and, of course, he wanted to please them. The party got mixed up with men and women toward the end. This allowed our close relatives to join the celebration. Adi made an appearance by being carried on one of his cousins' shoulders with the rest of his cousins and uncles. Men filled the dance floor and their wives followed to dance with them. My mother came running toward me to cover me with a white scarf shouting in my ear because of the loud music, "Adi requested that you cover yourself because the men have entered the hall."

I got provoked by what she did and yelled back at her, "But my dress is not that revealing. I don't want to cover my shoulders and dress on my wedding night."

She ignored me and waved Adi over to get me to dance with him.

Adi approached me and reached for my hand to pull me toward the dance floor. In return, I pulled him back close to me. "I don't want to cover myself. I don't want to ruin my dress with this scarf," I stated with an attitude.

"No man is allowed to see my wife's breasts. The dress is not ruined if you're concerned about that," he yelled in my ear.

I was distracted by the smell of his breath and ignored the fusty statement he made so I shrugged. "Your breath smells of alcohol. Did you drink?"

"I joined the guys for a couple of drinks. I only had two glasses of whisky," he specified.

I made my first mistake in this marriage and obeyed his order and kept the scarf on. I joined him on the dance floor and noticed the changed man he became after he had these couple of drinks. I wasn't the only one to note his changed behavior. He was too energetic, which made him carry me and start spinning in circles while everyone around us was clapping and cheering. His next move was placing me on one of the tables in the hall. I stood on the table fearing to fall down, and my father rushed toward me to make sure that I wouldn't fall off the table. Adi was too excited and continued clapping and dancing around me. All I was able to do was try to move my hands as a way of showing that I was dancing.

I was the bride covered in white while being dressed on the inside as a widow in black without realizing it. The joy I was feeling at my wedding blinded me from seeing what I was getting myself into. My family knew that a disaster would come out of this marriage and were concerned about me. Sadly, I chose to ignore their anxious stares and enjoy my night. It's weird how we choose the path to misery with full consent, with joy, and without any hesitation.

Victorious Night

Thirteen days full of stress passed by. He claimed that he was fine with the fact that I was still a virgin and that I could take as much time as I needed. As if this thing was an assignment and we had a deadline to finish it. Losing my virginity became a public issue that everyone was discussing. Whenever I visited my family, they would ask me if we had done IT.

We were trying every day. Whenever I would close my legs and push him away, he would become furious and jump off me with anger on his face. He would turn himself to the other side of the bed immediately, leaving me to burn on the inside till I cried myself to sleep. He would never turn back to hug me or comfort me. Rage would consume him, and he wouldn't think about anything other than his own failure. Kindness wasn't an option for him. His words were kind, but never his actions.

On our eighth day together as a married couple, I stood in the kitchen preparing dinner when he got an unexpected call from my mother. He was speaking to her freely around me until she asked him to go to a different room so she could speak to him privately.

He came out of the bedroom with a victorious look all over his face. His lips reached his ear with all the glory that my mother had filled him with.

"What did she want?" I asked.

He didn't take long to reply, "She asked me if we had had sex, and I answered her that we didn't. Then, she told me to grab you by the hair and force you to do it. She had said that you're spoiled and that I need to be firm with you."

My mother asked my husband to rape me. I stood in shock trying to digest what she said.

I didn't speak to my mother for a week. That lasted until my father called me and invited me to come over for lunch. Whenever I spoke to my father or saw him standing next to my mother, I would wonder how these two were able to live together for thirty years. They were the complete opposite of one another. She was dominant, loud, and selfish while he was peaceful, caring, and generous. She was the kind of lady that the neighbors would recognize by her loud voice anywhere they heard it because she used to scream at me and my siblings all the time. She cared about cleaning the house and keeping everything in order more than caring about our feelings. The first time that she actually kissed and hugged me was on my wedding night. On that night, she cried until her eyes got buried into her face. Her hugs and kisses felt foreign to my body. I couldn't feel her love.

I never believed that she loved my father; she had always seen him as an ATM machine. As long as he brought money to the house, he would receive her blessings, and if he asked her about the money she had taken from him, she would start yelling at him and saying that all the money he gave her was spent on the house. I recall the famous sentences that she had always used, *I wish I had spent the money on myself. I wish I was like the rest of the women who spend their days at the hair salons and spend a fortune on their clothes and makeup. Look at my hair and at me. This is all because I put your needs first. I sacrifice everything for you and your kids.*

My inhumane mother had a honeyed and moaning tone with strangers that would let them think that she was a sweet angel and that everyone around her was oppressing her. She had always excluded what she had done wrong in every story she told. The only events she ever mentioned would be about the bad actions that others had taken, but she never mentioned what she had done to receive such treatment. All the while my poor father had always been lost and tried hanging onto two ropes at the same time, with one rope connecting to his fed-up children and another to his barbarous, cruel wife. He didn't want to let go of either rope, hoping that he could tie them together again. Whenever he tried to pull both ropes closer to each other, his hands would open wider than before. His attempts gave him bleeding hands only.

As always, my mother satisfied others by hurting us. She cared about her image in front of her son-in-law rather than caring about the harm she was causing me. As expected, she asked me about my sacred virginity after we finished lunch and asked if we had done it. I lied and said that we did to keep her hurtful words away from me. She didn't believe me and asked for details. "Did you bleed? And did you save the proof of your virginity as I had taught you? I have given you the white kerchief for this purpose." I ignored what she said by saying that I didn't want to discuss it with her and shifted back to sit with the rest of the family to avoid this conversation.

We spent five days in Paris, returned to Jerusalem on day six, and he went back to his photo sessions on the same day we arrived home. I spent half of my time alone during the rest of the vacation which was supposed to feel like heaven before I returned to work. He used to always tell me that *a professional photographer never says no to a client or declines an offer. If I start postponing sessions and say that I cannot make it to their occasions, my clients will give up on me and find someone new.*

My first day at work was all about me and my marriage. My colleagues had a gathering in the teachers' room to congratulate me on my wedding. Yasmina who had recently become one of my close friends stood up and started reading out loud while holding a gift card in her hand: *To the most beautiful girl in this school, to the sensitive woman who is not afraid to seek help when she is in need, to the warm and powerful teacher that can affect her students with her great heart.* She stopped reading and looked at me, saying, "To the cool teacher that has a sense of humor that only her students can get. I think they laugh at your jokes to get good grades but it doesn't matter as long as they make you think that you're funny!"

Everyone started laughing and I threw a pencil at her for mocking my hilarious jokes. She continued reading with a smile of satisfaction on her face, "We hope that your dear husband will be the support system that you can rely on, and we wish you both a life full of happiness and love." I received hugs from my female coworkers and handshakes from my male colleagues. I waited till everyone left before I opened the gift card. It had the signatures of the teachers who contributed the money hidden inside the gift card.

I finished all the classes I had and waited for Yasmina to finish her meeting with the principal. Yasmina was the mother of everyone at the school—she put aside what she wanted for the sake of others. She used to give us great pieces of advice but never followed them herself. She was too afraid to hurt people's feelings by doing what would make her more comfortable.

She ran toward me with her arms wide open yelling, "Here is our beautiful bride." She sat next to me on a wooden bench and started asking me about the first two weeks of marriage. I was too shy to tell her that I didn't finish my sexual task with my husband. What could I have said? How could I have told her that we were having all sorts of sexual intimacy without intercourse? Who would understand that I allowed him to make me reach orgasm and didn't dare to let him put his penis inside of me? How could I be horny and not crave wanting to know what actual sex feels like? I didn't feel that it was appropriate to tell her that he managed to turn me on while rubbing his penis against my clitoris. I couldn't mention that I was able to give him a blow job and be fine with all sexual forms except for the main interaction. Instead of discussing the dilemma I was drowning in, I complained about the fact that I was alone most of the time.

I got off the bus and stopped by a supermarket that was close to my house to get some ingredients I needed for the dish I wanted to cook. My phone started ringing while I was paying for the groceries. As soon as I grabbed my phone out of my purse, I saw that it was Adi calling. He called to tell me that he would meet me at the house in an hour. I mentioned that I would try to have lunch ready by the time he was home. He responded that he had already eaten with one of his friends. *Don't bother to cook for me—please go ahead and make lunch for yourself. You need to eat as well. You need to get used to having cooked meals for you at home even if I don't join you.*

I couldn't scream or be angry at him in public even though I had fire coming out of my brain. I wanted a meal with my husband and he was telling me to never count him in any of my food plans.

I stood outside the supermarket with my phone in my hand and started typing, "You're no longer single, Adi, you have me in your life now. I am supposed to be your partner. The least you can do is join me once a day for a meal. Start putting me in your daily schedule for a change." I picked up the bags that were on the ground around me and started walking home while ignoring my phone which started ringing after sending this message.

When I got to the house, I unlocked my phone to read the text he had sent. "I married you because I think you're the perfect partner for me. Please don't get mad. I'll be home in half an hour. This is all because I am still not used to eating at home. I need some time to adjust."

We had built a habit of kissing and hugging each other every time he walked into the house, and as a sign of rebellion, I didn't run this time toward the door like always. He knew that he had to do something special to earn a kiss or a hug. He started hugging me from behind while I was facing the kitchen counter. I kept on pushing him away telling him to go and continue his meal with his beloved friend. "I don't want to kiss my hairy friend. I want to kiss you. My beautiful and delicious wife. The one that has the smell of a goddess." He tried to seduce me.

"You need to start having me as a priority. Same as I do you," I stated.

"My main priority right now is to throw you on the bed and take off your clothes. We're just going to have a nap, nothing more than sweet and harmless sleep. Even if I try to seek something more, I won't succeed." He teased me.

He stood behind me and pushed me toward the bedroom with his arms wrapped around my shoulder, and with his chin lying on my right shoulder. He shrank between my arms, leaving all the space that was left on the bed unused. He held my ear between his lips whispering, "I need to resolve the issues I have with your neck."

"What issues?" I giggled.

He replied to my question by licking my neck starting from my ear and leading his way down toward my breasts. I had always enjoyed foreplay; it was the part that never terrified me.

He gently lifted his body and laid it on mine. He started moving his penis on my stomach and then shifted to my private area. He reached for my anus with his fingers. Aiming for the target hole with his genital so he wouldn't make any mistakes by digging into the wrong area. I realized that the final moment had come to an end, "Please let's postpone this, we said that we'd only take a nap." I chickened out.

He ignored my request since he had a goal to achieve. For him, this was a task that needed to be crossed from his to-do list. I started screaming, begging him to stop while he had already started his attempt to slide his genital inside me. I tried to push him away, but he was able to nail my arms above my head using his hands. I couldn't understand if he was fucking me or if his attempt was going to be wasted away like the previous attempts. I couldn't know because I had never experienced sex.

He asked me to hold on for a few more seconds while I asked him to stop what he was doing. "Please stop I am in pain! I cannot stand this anymore!" I didn't realize that I was weeping like a baby until I cried this sentence out loud.

He pushed his penis harder inside me for one last time before he jumped off my body. He realized that this time he had succeeded and actually fucked me. This turn of events made him yell at me because he didn't see any blood leaking down my thighs. "Are you fucking kidding me? Is this some kind of a game you're playing?"

My husband accused me of being a whore; he doubted that I was a virgin, and he thought that I had been lying to him for the past couple of weeks to hide a secret. Men in our society usually divorce their wives for such a reason and would make a big scandal out of it. They would take their wives to a doctor to test if the hymen had been broken before, and if they proved that the girl they married wasn't a virgin, they would return her to her family, shaming the family for having a whore among them.

I yelled back at him. "Get away from me," and ran toward the bathroom to grab toilet paper. When I wiped my vagina with the toilet paper, blood covered it.

Adi was standing behind me observing everything that I was doing. I returned to the bed and grabbed a towel to wipe my vagina one more time. "Is this my period?" I foolishly asked. I was too shocked and terrified by what had happened. He felt the blood and started sensing the red texture by moving it between his thumb and his index finger. The victorious smile was on his face one more time. "Don't be silly—it is because we actually did it this time."

He tried to come closer to me, but I pushed myself away from him. "I hate you; I don't want to see your face! You actually accused me of being a whore. Don't you dare come near me!"

"Honey, I didn't accuse you of anything. I was just overwhelmed with what had happened. I really felt that I had it inside of you this time. We should celebrate this, not have a fight," he proudly uttered.

"I hate you. I hate what you've done to me," I cried.

My sentence made him laugh as if he had won a trophy, ignoring the fact that he had hurt me physically and emotionally.

His joy made me disregard his awful reaction and forced me to go with the flow. Love at this moment made me blind. I didn't want to see that I had married an uncivilized person who still treats women as a product that shouldn't be opened prior to marriage. I understood the reason behind the fear I had before and how overprotective I was over my genitals. I was one hundred percent sure that I was a virgin, but I was terrified not to bleed for some reason. Unfortunately, he had proved my theory. If I hadn't bled that night, he would've made a big deal out of it, and our celebration would've been a mourning.

The Triangle and the Square

I loved an average-looking man; he was even less than average. My husband wasn't good-looking, or handsome. I hate the sound of my words when I spill out this fact. Whenever we were out in public, people would stare at us as if they saw a triangle that was in love with a square. Many people commented on my husband's looks. Some would say to my face, *Why did you marry him? You're way prettier than him. I don't know how you fell in love with him. Love must be really blind.* Others would whisper it behind my back.

I wanted to hurt these people for saying this about him. I would really get upset and defensive whenever someone would call him ugly. I used to tell him that he was the most handsome man in the whole world. He would laugh and say, "Don't exaggerate. We both know that it's a lie."

I would look at him with passion and say, "You're the most handsome guy to me. This is how I see you and I don't care how others rank handsome men."

Adi knew how much I loved Mohammad Hamaki. He used to get jealous every time I stated this fact. One time we were driving the car and a song by Hamaki came on the radio. I spontaneously turned the volume up, and my eyes were immediately filled with joy. Unfortunately, we got to the house before the song was over, and Adi was thrilled to turn off the engine to stop the song. When I looked at him to demonstrate my frustration, I was able to see how provoked he was. "At least let us finish the song!" I said.

"We can call it good timing. I am glad we got home. You cannot love someone more than you love me and your eyes should sparkle like this only for me," he shrugged.

"You can't compare how I feel about you to the excitement I get over a song. His love songs remind me of you most of the time. Therefore, you need to be filled with joy when I listen to his happy songs and flattered when I send you one of his makeup songs when we're angry at each other," I explained.

Part of me was pleased to witness his jealousy. Usually, it would take a lot of effort to unleash the jealous monster that was hiding inside of him. Getting words out of his mouth became a hard task ever since we got married.

On June 6, 2018, he told me that he had seen an ad on Facebook announcing the dates of Hamaki's concerts in Jordan. "Will you be able to ask for leave from your work?" This is how far he could get with surprises and romance. He would ask directly and would use my permission to do something nice. At that moment, he made me forget how upset I was because he didn't know my favorite food or my favorite color.

I jumped and landed on his lap as a sign of agreement. "You don't even have to ask. Yes, Yes, and a thousand yes. I love you so much."

Later that night, we stopped by his parents' house. It didn't take him long to announce our trip to Jordan. His mother's face didn't seem so pleased when she said, "Why didn't you tell me earlier? I would've planned to come with you. Your uncle had been nagging all summer begging me to come visit." It was a way to make him feel guilty and to remind him that he should always consider her in his plans. They had a strong bond that made him feel obliged all the time to compensate for whatever wrong his father was doing to her. He felt the urge to make it up for her. I had been okay with this except for the jealousy part that his mother overwhelmed me with. He offered for her to join us and tried to convince her that it wasn't too late for her to consider going on this trip with us.

She declined his offer and turned her head toward me and said with a sigh, "Next time I'll go with my beloved daughter-in-law. I'll introduce her to all of our relatives there."

We checked into a five-star hotel and reserved a room for one night only. I offered to pay for half of the trip's expenses once we got into our room. He refused to take the money I had in my hands, "This time it's on me. Consider it a gift." I hugged him and thanked him for his sweet gesture. He gazed at me with a wicked smile and uttered, "I know how you can thank me."

"You know that you have a dirty look on your face, my dear husband?"

"You know me too well, my dear wife."

He squeezed my ass with his fist and started kissing me on the lips. I was able to determine how horny he was based on the way he would kiss me. When the kiss included a tongue, it would mean that he would not take his hands off of me without ending it with sex, and if the kiss felt like a quick print on the surface of my lips, then it would mean that he was passing on a loving vibe. This time, his kisses were French mixed with some Arabian licking.

The hardest moment was waking up from the nap that followed the adventurous sex we had. If we wanted to get a good spot at the amphitheater, we had to get there the earliest we could. I learned my lesson the hard way, and I knew that I had to be gentle whenever I wanted to wake him up. I started kissing him on the forehead while whispering all the loving names I knew. I shifted toward his cheek calling him *Habibi'* then turned to his nose while uttering my love. I then went down to his chin murmuring 'my life' and ended it by leaving a last kiss on his neck while saying *Adi*. He heavily opened his eyes while his mouth gradually opened to say *Habibti*.

I was allowed to wear a short dress despite him hating the idea of having his wife wandering around a concert filled with guys from all over the Arab world. "You know that I don't like it when you wear short dresses or skirts in public."

"We're on a trip; can't you loosen up when we're outside Jerusalem?"

"The change of place doesn't mean that I can be ok with it. This is the last time that you wear such a dress."

"We'll negotiate this issue during our next trip."

"We're not going to negotiate this issue again. The case is closed."

I winked at him. "We'll see about that."

When we reached the Jerash amphitheater, I clung to his hand like a child afraid to lose his mother. I felt that he was my safety net, and I was certain that he would protect me despite the fact that I had never been in a situation to witness him defending me. I have no idea how I developed this blind trust. I think that I didn't want to believe or see otherwise. I built a perfect image for him in my head and made sure I blindfolded my eyes to protect myself from seeing anything that might shatter this image.

We waited for an hour before Hamaki showed up on stage. I kept track of every minute that would pass hoping that the upcoming minute would be the beginning of the show. The ray of hope made me wait for an entire hour without feeling any sort of boredom. When he finally appeared on stage, I kept on shouting as loud as I could, sang along to the lyrics, and clasped my hands together while swaying my body to the floating rhythm.

At the end of the concert, I wrapped my hand around Adi's waist from behind and leaned my head on his shoulder. He looked down at me and mouthed in my ear, "The party is not over yet; we have one more station to pass by." I looked back at him with confusion, asking for clarification. "I got us passes to go backstage and meet Hamaki in person. Don't forget that I have good connections."

"Are you for real?" I asked.

"You'll see for yourself in ten minutes. Let us first pass through the crowd, and we'll then meet your big star," he uttered with an arrogant smile.

We were able to sneak backstage successfully to see that Hamaki had fans taking pictures with him. Adi called him out as if he were a friend. Hamaki greeted Adi with a big smile in return. Adi pulled me after him to take a photo with the great singer. Adi jabbed himself between Hamaki and me, refusing to give me a chance to have a solo photo with him. His Middle Eastern masculinity prevented him from letting another man touch me, even if it was just for the sake of a picture.

Salma a Vampire Sucking Money Out of Men

Salma. The crazy, yet irresistible woman was a complex psychological mess. She would steal the essence of any room she would walk into. She was able to open conversations with anyone she met. She seemed confident despite the fact that she was damaged on the inside. Cursing the day she got married and swearing that she would never repeat the same mistake again was her thing, yet she was thrilled by the idea of having suitors fighting over her.

She used to narrate the events that caused her divorce to me in detail. It all started when her father forced her to marry her cousin. No one dared to have a say regarding this marriage, not even Adi. He was fifteen when she got engaged, and Salma was sixteen. A one-year difference between the two siblings shaped her as a woman and excluded him from turning into a man.

Whenever we gathered together without having a male presence among us, she would reveal events of her tragic story. *You know, I was disgusted by him. I couldn't stand him. When he used to come over to visit, I used to stay in my room and leave him with Adi and my father. When he would suggest going out together, I would bring Tala along with us. He hated the fact that I had my little sister attached to us every time we hung out together.*

He once followed me to the kitchen to kiss me, and instead of letting him kiss me, I asked him to leave me the fuck alone and break this terrible engagement. He got mad over the idea that I didn't want him and nodded his head like a decent man. I thought that he had the dignity to leave a girl that doesn't want him.

Do you know what he did in return? He went out to the living room to join my father. Five minutes later, I heard my father yelling my name as if a catastrophe had happened. I almost peed in my pants when I heard my name.

I knew that nothing good would come out of this screaming. I stood in front of both of them waiting for my trial. The coward didn't say a word—he let my father explain the situation. My father started weeping and lamented my shameful behavior. She stood up to imitate the way her father moved his body while wailing about what she had requested. *All of a sudden, he threw himself on the floor and started saying that he could not breathe and that his heart was hurting. I was able to feel that he was faking this to make me feel bad and change my mind. After all, I was raised by this man, and I know him very well.*

When I heard this for the first time, I stopped her to ask about her mother's reaction and if she defended her desire to break this engagement. My question was directed to Salma despite the fact that my mother-in-law was with us in the same room. She looked her mother in the eye and sighed heavily, "This old woman? She had never stood in the face of my father. She couldn't say anything that would conflict with the wishes of her beloved husband. She's a strong woman with everyone except my father." She laughed and expressed the situation by saying, "I think that love blinded her and made her weak." Her mother remained passive even when she heard this…confirming the facts that were uttered by her daughter.

I couldn't help, but think of how stupid this sentence was. If I were in her place, I wouldn't let anyone dare commit such a crime by letting my minor daughter marry someone she hates. I was afraid to judge her and feared that one day love might make me weak, too.

Her story was broken into parts; she would tell me the events separately on different occasions. One time, she was showing me her old engagement and wedding pictures. This made her reveal incidents of her sexual life with her ex-husband. *Doesn't he look like a mouse? I was ashamed of him and of the way he looked. I would hide from my classmates whenever I was with him so they wouldn't feel sorry for me. The most beautiful girl in their class married a mouse. I was the only blonde girl with colored eyes back then. Boys would fight over my attention, and I didn't want to ruin the image they had of me and start looking at me with pity for what I had settled for. Even the sex was horrible. I remember that I didn't let him touch me for days. He even cried once because I rejected him. In the end, he bought a soporific drug so I could sleep while he finished his thing. I lost my virginity while I was drugged asleep. At other times, I would stay still until he had orgasms and got his…out of me.*

The next time an event of her story was revealed was when we were out together in a coffee shop. Her mother was present listening to the story while commenting that her daughter had a tough experience.

He was too weak to stand in the face of his siblings and wanted to prove the theory they had about us wrong. They kept on telling him that I was in control of everything and that he should be the man in the relationship and stop listening to me. His sisters once cornered me in the stairwell and hit me with a metal tray on my head. I ran back to the house and called my father to rescue me from these monsters.

She stopped to ask me. "Did I mention to you that we all lived in the same building?"

She continued describing the misery she used to live in after she clarified this information to me. Nevertheless, she didn't go into detail regarding what happened when her father showed up for the rescue. I felt that this scene was deleted from her story for a reason. In the end, her father was the reason behind postponing the breakup of this marriage until she stayed married for eight years and had two boys.

Her father's reaction to what had been happening to her appeared in other stories she told. She mentioned that he used to make her apologize to her ex-husband's family even though they were the ones who mistreated her.

He made me apologize several times. Whenever they would do me wrong, he would come to kiss me on the forehead and beg me to say that I was sorry. He used to tell me that I was the youngest and that the youngest should respect the eldest. I cried myself to sleep whenever this happened. I felt that I had no dignity. The same thing happened over and over again till I became an actual adult and dared to say no to my father. When I refused to apologize, he started hitting himself on the head screaming that I would shame him.

The thing with Salma is that you sympathize with her character and the way she was mistreated, and then out of nowhere, her wicked acts shock you. She had put me in a paradoxical situation where I couldn't determine if I had to feel sorry for her or be afraid of her.

I expressed that I sympathized with Salma's story to Adi. He answered me saying, "You only heard her part of the story." Curiosity pushed me to ask for an elaboration on this sentence. He moved on to mention the missing parts of her tale. "My sister is not that innocent. Letting her marry that young was a complete mistake, and if I would go back in time I would help her change her destiny. However, she mistreated her husband and disrespected him. She treated him like an insect. No one would accept being treated that way. I heard several phone calls between them when she used to come over to visit us. She would start swearing at him and would curse his God."

I didn't want to believe him since I was convinced that her story was the correct one and this made me ask, "What about him not bringing food to the house? She said that he used to tell her that nothing was left from his salary and she was the one in charge of buying groceries."

He laughed and said, "And you believed her? His salary used to be transferred straight to her bank account. She controlled everything."

I cannot deny that he wasn't a real man and that he used to be affected by whatever anyone would tell him, and follow women's babbling words. That's who he was. He was weak, and he had to keep trying to prove that he wasn't.

"He and Salma were living in the same house but were lost in completely different places. She was ashamed of his job as a construction worker and considered it a stinky job. She wanted to live a fancy life in the high-class society while having a presentable husband. That all started when she continued her studies and began to notice the intellectual difference between them. She got herself a degree while he didn't even know how to read or write."

The divorced young lady who gave up her two sons was aiming to find an eligible rich suitor. She was living a conflicted story. On some days, she would scream at her sons and curse their god, and on other days, she would cry over the fact that they were living away from her. She thought that buying them clothes and expensive objects whenever they would come to visit her would make a great mom out of her. She treated her sons as visitors who would leave at the end of the day to return to their original house with their father and stepmother.

She was well aware of the fact that her family in general and her father in particular couldn't tolerate her boys' presence around the house. For her father, they were the stones that were holding his daughter down to the seabed. He was counting the seconds and days for her to get married again so she wouldn't dishonor him by having an affair with a man out of wedlock. He kept on bullying her regarding the way she dressed by saying that it was revealing. He tried to force her to wear the headscarf to cover her golden locks of hair. By this time, she had learned to fight back against his oppressiveness.

Hide and Seek

When Adi and I got engaged, people approached me to warn me about his father. They described him as a despicable human being who would do anything to win and get what he wanted. He was known for being one of the elders that practiced the tribal laws. The tribal laws were recognized as a way to help solve problems that occurred within the Arab communities to avoid seeking the help of the Israeli police. It was an alternative that was supposed to help the weak get their rights back. Instead, it became a corrupt system that gave men with no morals the power to make decisions that oppress innocent people.

These men would use the name of God and Islam in their speeches while having hidden goals. Many of them aim for one of the following reasons: getting bribes, making a name for themselves, sleeping around with mistreated women in return for representing them, and getting their rights back…the list of benefits they strive for is long and unethical. It's rare to have men among them who would want to help only for the sake of achieving justice. It's usually for personal objectives.

A while ago, I heard a story about one of these men. A woman who was mistreated by her husband needed someone to represent her divorce case among the elders. She went to a man asking him to represent her and claim her rights and child support. The price he asked for was her body. He asked her to sleep with him in return for this favor.

Another case was when a young man was killed in a fight that happened between two families. Each family had men representing their case. The killers had someone to speak for them and defend them, and the same was the case with the ones who had lost their boy. The killers approached the guy who was representing the other family and paid him more money so he could manipulate things in their favor. At the end of the tribal trial, the man who was supposed to defend the young man's life started giving justifications for the one who had committed the crime. He settled for the money that the abusers offered in return for the murderer's life. The victims didn't get justice because of the corruption that surrounded this rotten system, and the murderer got away with his act by letting his whole family pay for what he had done.

Adi's father was known to be one of these people. The one who would turn things around to get what he wanted. I witnessed several events involving him that showed him as a man with a PhD in acting and lying. He was able to shed tears whenever he had to, and he would act his way out of anything. He strutted the streets as if he were an honorable man while he had quite a temper around his family.

I recall the night I was around Adi's family for dinner when my father-in-law received a call from his brother. He was dressed and about to get out when his phone rang. It seemed to be a normal conversation at the beginning until his brother told him that he was coming over to visit him with his wife and kids. My father-in-law responded with nothing but lies. "Oh, I wish you had told me earlier. I am at a funeral now and won't be home soon. It's the funeral of Abu Majed Saleh."

His brother answered him saying, "We need two minutes and we'll be in front of the building's main gate. I'll call your wife to open the gate for us. Maybe we'll see you when you get back home if luck would be on our side."

Adi's father started jumping up and down cursing God's name. His head was about to explode from the rage that was inside him. He yelled at his wife uttering, "He'll be here in two minutes. What should I do? People are expecting me in Ramallah. May God be cursed for what I got myself into."

He got his car keys and moved his car to the building that was facing the building where they lived. He asked Salma to call him once his brother entered the house so he could escape his way out without letting his brother see him. His brother called my mother-in-law telling her that they were in front of the gate.

"Stall him till I make it to the other side and hide in the car. Tell him that you cannot find the keys to the main gate." He asked his wife to lie for him, and she did it without hesitation. I looked at Salma to find her laughing out of embarrassment. I laughed back since I felt as if I were in a Tom and Jerry movie. I had to see my 60-year-old father-in-law hide in a car to make sure that his brother wouldn't think of him as a liar and get to the gathering he was heading to. Both his wife and daughter did as he wished, and the James Bond movie scene was soon over when he got his way out of the parking space where he was hiding.

I never told Adi about the hide-and-seek scene that I'd witnessed, but he knew that I was well aware of the type of man his father was. He was able to sense that I never liked his father. He was ok with it as long as I was treating his father with respect. He was fond of his father and considered him an idol deserving a statue of his own. He thought of him as a man of steel that nothing could beat. I wondered how he was able to love the monster that abused him as a child and forced his sister into marrying someone at a very young age that she didn't love. This was one of the problems in the society I lived in—the monster gets idolized while the good man gets crushed and humiliated.

Neglected

He wanted me to meet his friends. He felt the urge to let me into his loud and outrageous world. Assuming that I'd fall in love with it and would want to be part of it.

I was left alone in the middle of a party he took me to. He entered the room, ignoring the fact that I was standing next to him. I followed him until my dignity stopped me and forced me to sit on a window ledge. I pretended to be okay despite the fact that I was surrounded by strangers, with my husband running around forgetting all about me. He came toward me holding a glass of whiskey that had two rocks of ice in it while he had his hands around a girl's shoulder. He introduced me to Jessica as his lovely wife while giving his attention to the unlovely Jessica. After a few seconds, they both ignored my existence and walked toward their other friends.

I waited for 33 minutes and then decided to walk away.

I walked home with my heels on. I didn't want to disturb the happy and drunk jerk who forgot he had brought his wife with him.

My inner parts were eaten by my aching heart. I was defeated by my own sorrow.

I laid down on our bed waiting for him with the light of hope coming out of my phone. I scrolled down my Facebook home page without paying attention to any of the posts. I woke up the next day trying to reach his pillow with my hand hoping to catch his flesh on it, but he wasn't there.

I found my jerk husband dead asleep on the sofa with his clothes on.

I stood in the kitchen and made breakfast for one as a sign of rebellion. He woke up to find me eating by myself.

"Why didn't you call me to join you?" He asked.

I stayed silent and didn't reply.

He got closer to my face to ask, "What's wrong?"

I didn't answer and kept my head down, staring at the plate with fried eggs.

"I am speaking to you, look at me!" he demanded.

I looked up at him eye-to-eye, feeling his breath on my face, and mouthed, "Nothing, nothing is wrong."

"Then why are you eating alone? Usually, you call for me when you make breakfast. Don't start saying nothing is wrong when apparently everything is."

I kept looking straight into his face with rage coming out of my eyes. He continued asking with a gentle tone, feeling the volcano about to erupt out of me. "What's wrong, Habibti?" Calling me sweetheart didn't help tame the beast that was crawling slowly out of me. I started my sentence in a calm voice and ended up shouting, "Everything you did yesterday was wrong. You fucking forgot about me at the party! You didn't even call to check on me. I hope you had fun with your blonde bitch! Did you even notice that I was gone? I bet your bitch noticed that I was no longer there and was thrilled by that."

I was on fire while he was swimming in a pool of ice. "You cannot call her a bitch. Why did you even leave?"

"She's a bitch! How dare you forget what's important and focus on what I call her. You care about the names I call other people, but you don't care about how I feel?" I yowled.

"Why didn't you interact with other people? I didn't force you to leave. You didn't even tell me that you're leaving." He tried to put the blame on me.

I kept on mumbling bad things to myself when I got away from my chair to clean up the table. He followed me and stood behind me trying to hug me. I kept on pushing his hands away from my body. He thought that he could erase what he did with a hug and a kiss. I turned back at him with bursting tears, "You ignored me; you kept on speaking to her as if I wasn't there. She didn't even respect that you had your wife with you. She just dragged you away."

I got an apology out of him, and he kept on kissing me until I hugged him back. "Don't you ever do that to me again. I will kill you if you do it one more time." I threatened him while he was overjoyed by my jealousy. Being between his arms didn't make it up, but I couldn't step away. I needed this hug and these kisses yesterday, but I had settled for them today instead.

It wasn't long until he did it again. He spent most of the weekdays away and would usually return home after I had collapsed and gone to bed. When he used to return home late, he would wake me up for our usual sex rituals and then leave me wide awake, smitten with him. An orgasm lasting for ten seconds made me think that all of our problems that we had ten hours prior could go away and disappear. I was delusional, thinking we had a great life together since our sex life felt astonishing to me.

The Snail and Its Shell

I was happily, and slowly, stabbing myself in the gut whenever I remembered every sip of love I had ever received from him, I was attached to our late-night cuddles. When he used to join me in bed, he would crawl slowly toward my side of the bed to hug me. This gesture helped me maintain the love I had in my heart for him, despite all of the fights that we would have during the day and despite the fact that he wasn't present with me most of the time. The act of shrinking between my arms like a snail crawling back into its shell for safety and comfort made me feel the love he had for me, and the fact that he felt comfortable to close his eyes and be lost in my shell, tickled my inner soul. At the same time, his acts during his conscious times would ruin this moment for me.

My husband wished to be someone he wasn't, and he couldn't get out of the mental damage that his father caused him as a child. It was similar to wearing a shirt that you despise and not being able to change it because someone in the past deprived you of the right to choose new clothes that would actually fit. He hated this shirt and couldn't adjust to anything else. He got stuck and feared leaving it thinking that he would never find something that would match the color of his skin.

I sympathized with his case because I saw the struggle he was having. I saw a different side to his character when he was around different people. It was as if he was able to change colors around the different people he had in his life. If he were around his intellectual friends and artists, he would try to sound polite and creative. The selection of words differed from one person to another. His true color was mostly shown around his cousins and family. He couldn't hide it. If one of his family members would trigger his angry side, he would start jumping up and down cursing the existence of the universe and the Creator of this damned world. I noticed how his leg would be twitching in the presence of his father as if he were trying to suppress the angry monster that was hiding inside him. The monster disagreed and agreed with every word his father would say. On the other hand, he was the brother that was feared, yet loved by his sisters.

I got a chance to witness all of the shades of his character. He was a complex human being who was able to love and yet spread harm at the same time.

Cold Affection

Wine and Entrecote steak were in the bag he held in his hand when he entered the house. "Are you in the mood for a feast cooked by the great chef Adi Makhlouf?" He proudly asked.

"If you're cooking, then the answer is a definite yes, my love," I answered with my hands wrapped around his waist. I sat on a chair in the kitchen and observed him while he was cooking. He stopped to open a bottle of wine and offered me to try it. I took one sip of the glass and all of a sudden my eyes and lips shrank because of the taste I experienced for the first time in my life.

He laughed at the reaction I had and uttered, "I guess your drinking experience is over after this."

"It tastes like an expired and sour grape juice," I sighed. I raised my hand and declared, "However, I want to try to get tipsy. I learned this word from movies, and I want to know how it feels. I'll force myself into drinking one glass or two until I reach the stage of tipsiness."

I closed my eyes whenever I drank from the glass I held in my hand and tried to swallow the wine quickly before I felt its taste in my mouth. He noticed that every time I would take a sip, I would drink as much as I could of the wine to get the feeling I was aching to feel. This made him advise me to slow down. "I have a goal to achieve and if I don't do what I am doing now, then I'll be disgusted by the taste and not dare to drink from it. You take care of the cooking, and I'll be your assistant who will be drinking while doing the dishes and cleaning the mess you're creating. Each of us should stick to our duties, please," I replied with enthusiasm.

We sat at the dining table with two pieces of steak for each one of us. We were enjoying our meal while discussing the events that had shaped our day. I started to feel a little dizzy so I stood up to feel the sensation of being tipsy. I played a slow song and asked him to join me for a dance. He hesitated at the beginning and told me to get back to the table to finish my meal. I forced him to stand up by dragging him away from his comfort zone to hold me in his arms and dance. I was able to sense that he felt that my actions were strange compared to what he was used to. He couldn't be spontaneous and needed someone to guide him through the steps of such unrestrained entertainment.

"I kind of like the feeling I have at the moment. I feel that my body is floating while being anchored to the ground at the same time. I finally experienced one of the mysteries I was dying to feel. Next time, you need to let me get drunk so we can see how a drunken Saba would behave," I mumbled.

"You're referring to yourself as a third person. I think we're halfway there," he muttered in return.

"No. I am still aware of what is happening, and I can control my behavior. I am not drunk," I replied.

The wine made me sleepy and I ended the night by falling asleep on the sofa until Adi approached me to move me to bed.

That night I managed to force him to dance with me and forget about the chains he wrapped himself with.

I was a hopeless romantic who thought that our life would be pinkish and full of rainbows. I kept on trying to keep the flavor of love present. On the other hand, he stopped trying to win my love by pressing the pause button when our engagement days were over. Whenever I would tell him that he changed, he would state, "People don't stay the same after they get married. Married couples care about the responsibilities they have."

I remember jumping up and down next to him on the sofa showing him the silver pen he gave me as a gift when we had started dating to remind him of the thoughtful gestures he used to do. "You got me this with my name engraved on it when you knew that I love to write." His response resembled a complimentary smile, and he shifted his head back to the TV screen.

The heat of our marriage was extinguished before we even had babies or finished a year together as a married couple. I wanted to change the nature of Adi's character and turn him into a compassionate man when he wasn't even close to being one. Hope made me wish that the lion would turn vegetarian and stop preying on other animals. I was fighting against Mother Nature; I was chasing a light that was leading me to a dead end.

Dirty Bed Sheets

My hip was swaying from side to side. I was weeping my misery out of me while dancing to his favorite song. I belly-danced till my knees collapsed. I was forced to dance to his drunken soul while mine was fading. He was neither sober nor aware of what he was doing to me. I fell down, my mascara covering my face with blackness, and yet he didn't give up on me. He held me by the hand and dragged me to bed.

I yelled, 'No' ten times in a row. I was too tired to fight him, and he was too strong to notice that I was falling apart in front of him. My husband raped me until he fainted from his drunken orgasm. The sheets were smudged by the semen that was sliding from my defeated body.

I crawled to reach the bathtub. The water failed to cover neither my bruises nor my pain.

He woke up the next day to find me asleep in the water; he held my wet body and dried it with a dirty towel. After all, a lot of things in our house needed cleaning.

"Saba, what happened?"—He asked a simple question that needed a furious answer. I looked down at him trying to give a reaction to what I was feeling. I wanted to hit him, scratch him, or even stab him. Instead, I stayed silent and calm while he started begging for forgiveness.

I was well aware of what was going to happen. It was as if I was late for work, and the clock kept on ticking forward while I was still on the road. I knew that I wouldn't be able to make it on time, but as each minute passed by I would tell myself that I still had four minutes left. Then, the four minutes would be over, and I would miss work. False hope and denial smashed what was left of me. I thought that I still had a chance to find the good in Adi. Whenever he did me wrong, I would say I still have time tomorrow to change this, but when tomorrow came, he stayed the same.

I used to wonder why all these mistreated women stayed mired in their misery. Then a time came when I understood why—they were smitten by their loved ones. They kept on hoping that the abuse wouldn't happen ever again and that they had a supernatural power that could help them change the person they loved. While the act of abuse is repeated, there is a string of hope dangling from it.

He let go of me and sat in the corner of the bathroom with his hands on his head. He realized that his hug wasn't accepted even though I didn't object to it, but he was alert and noticed that my hands were loose and were hanging down my body. The silence that permeated the room was pierced by his words, "Do you remember our first date?" He didn't care to have an answer to his question since he was too ashamed to look at me. He moved on to narrate the events that led to our big official date.

You were wearing a red jacket and had a wintery black dress beneath it. I was going to skip attending that dinner with you and your colleagues, but the principal of the school insisted that I should. I bet you're wishing that I went home that night and didn't bump into you.

During the afternoon, I watched you prepare your students for their big play. You were rehearsing their lines with them. I loved the way you spoke English, by the way.

The whole afternoon passed by and you didn't notice me as if I was invisible to you. I had pictures taken of all the activities that were done on that day. The most spectacular picture among them all was of you standing backstage with your hands stapled together while observing the performance of your students. I was afraid that you or anyone in the audience would notice that I was stalking you with the lens of my camera.

I prayed to God that night that the empty seat next to me would be taken by you. God answered my prayers and you came running late to sit next to me. You asked for permission to sit in it when it was reserved for you since the beginning.

You smiled at me and asked, "Aren't you Adi Makhlouf, the photographer?" I smiled back and confirmed the information. You stated with enthusiasm, "You're someone famous, and I should take advantage of that. Can I take a picture with you? If I look good in it, I'll post it on Facebook."

I couldn't do anything but take advantage of this moment so I answered you with confidence, "No, you can't...unless you tag me in it. And you cannot do so because I am not on your friends list." Your face turned red for a moment so I continued being charming and seized your phone out of your hand to add myself as a friend on Facebook. It was a risky move, but I am glad I did it. In the end, I was rewarded with having my picture taken with you and with you proudly posting it on your profile with my name tagged to it.

Conjuring events from the past didn't help me at that moment. I stopped him by asking him to take me to bed. He carried me out of the bathroom and placed me on the bed. "Leave me the hell alone now," I requested.

He opened a door of memories that made me recall our first date.

~Seven a.m. on a Sunday morning. I had never woken up that early on a Sunday before. It felt different, the sky and the atmosphere were yellowish. Same as Adi's eye color. I had my hair up and messy in a bun, luckily the weather was not as messy as my hair. It was still freezing, but rain was not part of the plan for that day. I had a quick shower before my mom had woken up. I did not want her to suspect my strange behavior that day. When I went out of the bathroom, I accidentally bumped into Sami's shoulder. I was terrified of my own brother for the first time in my life. I was paranoid enough to think that he would know why I was up that early. Fortunately, he was sleepy enough and didn't notice my weird behavior. He just walked past me saying: "watch where you're going, idiot." It was completely normal, he forgot that Sunday was my day off or even the fact that it was a Sunday.

I rushed into my room and straightened my hair; it was naturally straight, but I had to make sure that everything would be perfect that day. I gazed at myself in the mirror, moved my hands between the locks of my black hair, stared right into my green wide eyes, and mumbled to myself, "Is this even real?"

My phone rang.

"Will you at least give me more details?" It was Yasmina.

"I told my mom that I am going to spend the whole day with you. I promise I'll be back by nine. Don't answer any of my mom's calls, and if anything dangerous happens even though I doubt that it will, just call me." I assured her that everything would be fine while I was finishing drawing my eyeliner.

Tel Aviv Port was almost empty, and everyone was hiding indoors because of the cold. I looked around me, but he wasn't there. I did not call. I just waited calmly gazing at the sea. My hands were bleak lying on the wooden barrier that was separating land and sea. I heard the sound of a picture being taken from behind. It was him. "As I imagined, I got you the perfect shot. I am sorry for keeping you waiting. Why are you standing in the cold?" This guy did not know how to start a normal conversation.

"I don't mind the cold," I replied.

He walked toward me in slow motion till he reached me. I glanced up at his amber eyes that were hiding behind his transparent glasses and asked, "What's the plan?"

We walked toward a seafood restaurant that was located at the end of the port. He reached for my hand, but I refused to give in. This made him smile out of embarrassment.

The waitress approached us with the menu. I tried to choose something on my own but failed. "Choose something special for me," I uttered.

He had it all figured out. "That should be easy; we'll go for the lobster." He moved on and asked tensely, "It wouldn't be a problem if I ordered a bottle of wine, would it?"

I had a big problem with that, but did not know how to reject it. Instead, I approved his request. Adi ordered and the waitress wrote everything down. I added to his order, "And a glass of lemonade, please."

"Have you ever drunk alcohol before?" He asked as if he did not already know the answer to his question.

"I have never even tasted it," I announced.

He asked if I would like to try it. I rejected the offer in a polite tone. I was still aware of my actions and didn't let him seduce me. I watched him swallow his wine one sip after another counting the number of glasses he had even though I tried not to. He drank three glasses and poured the fourth. I was not fully aware of my facial expressions, but it was clear to him that I was uncomfortable. "What's the matter?" He asked. I chose to say that nothing was wrong; I did not want to ruin my date by pointing out that I wasn't familiar with alcohol. I did not want to be the conservative girl even though I was. He was not convinced by my answer so he grabbed my hand, kissed it, and breathed into it saying: "You can tell me. I don't bite."

I nervously spitted out the words as if I were confessing a crime. "You drank so much and soon you'll be driving."

Surprisingly, he pushed the fourth glass away and said, "It feels good to have someone worry about me. You can tell me anything you want. I want us to lose the awkwardness. If I annoy you with anything, feel free to state it out loud."

I escaped the situation by leaving the table to go to the bathroom. I needed a five-minute break to get myself together. I whispered to myself, "Saba, just be you. If he doesn't accept you for who you are, then he's not worth your time."

I managed to bring out the fun character that was hidden at first because of all the tension, I had surrounded myself with. I got back to the table with a new spirit. "So, do you like cheese?" I asked in a serious tone.

"Why?" He replied with a question.

"I remembered a scene from a movie where the main character asks his friend for advice about how to speak to someone he likes. The friend tells him to say something casual such as asking if the girl likes cheese, and that would lead them to have a real conversation. Since we're in a weird situation, I would like to ask if you like cheese."

"I think the perfect answer would be that I like you more than cheese," he responded.

"Impressive! I think this would lead to an excellent conversation," I bubbled.

The fun was over, and the goal of reaching a fine conversation was achieved.

"Now, it's my turn. Do you like me?" He asked with a serious face.

I tried to be smart and ignore his question, "It's too early for your turn. I am in the lead now. Where are you originally from?"

"You're changing the subject. Do you like me, Saba?" He asked again.

"If I say that I do, would you answer my questions?" I asked.

"If you'll say that just to have the answers, then I don't need to hear it that way," he declared.

I gave him the satisfaction he was searching for by confessing that I liked him back. ~

Adi came back to the room with a freshly-squeezed orange juice. He placed the glass of juice on the nightstand and sat next to me. He threw his upper body at me while his lower body lay along the side of the bed. He breathed in my ear, "I am sorry."

The Souvenir

Men keep on convincing us and themselves that they are right. They would cheat on you and still convince you that they didn't. Their determination to show their side of the story as the true part would make you think that you were hallucinating and make you doubt the evidence you have in your own hands.

We were having dinner at a restaurant viewing all of Jerusalem from its garden. We glanced at the shining lights that were coming out of the buildings at nighttime, but the most visible light was coming out of the Golden Dome of the Rock. This historical piece of Islamic architecture seemed like a queen surrounded by her followers—everything was aimed toward her and everyone was drooling to take over her.

The waitress brought us the check and left. I looked away to avoid the awkwardness of him having to pay for our meals. I glanced to see something fall from his wallet, I leaned down under the table to capture a pornographic picture. It had a woman and a man that appeared to be locals. I was able to guess that it was not a picture from the internet. It looked very original. I was able to tell that he took this picture. "You never told me that you take such pictures."

He misled me as usual and claimed that it belonged to a friend who does these photo sessions as a profession. He moved on to say, "He gave it to me as a souvenir." I felt that something fishy was going on behind my back. I stayed silent making him think that the case was closed even though I prepared myself to start an investigation of my own.

The next morning, I sneaked out of bed at 5:00 a.m. His phone was plugged into the charger on the nightstand as usual. I never dared to touch his phone or look into it before that moment. He was too secretive regarding what he had on it, and this made him set boundaries for holding each other's phones. He once told me that one phone shouldn't be shared by two people, and we both should respect each other's privacy. He would make a moral statement for his own good. I reached for his phone while observing his chest go up and down with closed eyes. I couldn't help, but imagine his eyes getting wide open to catch me stealing his phone. It made my hands shake and my heartbeats reach the sky.

I stood in the living room trying to remember the password. I observed him type it whenever he used to open his phone but wasn't sure if I had it right in my mind. I tried once, twice, and feared that the third time would lock it. Therefore, I thought that if the third time wouldn't work then it would be a sign from God to let it go and just trust my husband. God had another plan for me and helped me remember the numbers on the third try.

He had unread messages in his WhatsApp chats. Three were from his family group and two were from his high school friends' group. I scrolled down the messages to find a conversation with a girl called Samia, two windows down was another chat with a girl called Aseel, and one more with another female called Yasmeen. I decided to start reading Samia's messages since she was the most recent one on his WhatsApp. It was obvious that he had erased their old messages since their conversation was smooth and based on previous discussions.

Samia Derbas

S: Guess who I ran into at the Wedding :)
A: Who?
S: Ahlam! I didn't expect to see her there
A: Forget about Ahlam.
I want to see how you looked at the wedding, gorgeous
S: We only took group photos
A: Don't start making excuses just send me what you have;)

She sent him six pictures. Not two, not three, not even four. No, she sent six.

S: Are you relieved now?
A: You look stunning as usual, dear
I'm sure everyone had their eyes on you

I started taking screenshots of the sentences that provoked me and kept on reading.

S: Why aren't you replying to my messages, Adi?
A: Sorry, I got busy this week
You know I wouldn't do this on purpose
S: It's not the first time. At least reply when you can. Don't keep me hanging.
A: Don't make a big deal out of it
It's not as if I didn't reply to a life-or-death text
S: I take time out of my day to check on you
And you cannot reply saying that you're doing fine?
A: How have you been? Everything is ok with you?
S: Yes, all is well. I miss you!

He did it again. He left her hanging. He didn't reply to her last message as if he was playing the cat and mouse game with her. He flirted with her at some point and then wouldn't reply to her messages leaving her stuck in the air after getting all her attention. He made her think that she mattered to him and at the same time he was playing hard to get.

I moved on to Aseel's window and wished that I hadn't read what it had.

Aseel Saleh

I miss your face, Adood

He sent her a picture of himself lying on the bed after he received this message.

Now let me see you

She didn't hesitate to send a picture of herself either, and when I moved on through the chat, I found several pictures that were exchanged among them.

A: Why is your upper lip red?
AS: I got it waxed

Did you know that Yasmeen is in Jerusalem?
A: Are you fucking kidding me?
The sweet angel is in the holy land?
AS: Hahaha you crack me up, Adi
Yes, she is. Your sweet angel
A: The softest girl on earth is in the neighborhood
AND I DIDN'T KNOW
I'll check on her to see if she'll say anything
AS: Good luck, Handsome!

His conversation with his sweet angel Yasmeen was shockingly polite. He offered to give her a tour around Jerusalem since she came all the way from Haifa. Yasmeen was assigned to work as a temporary nurse at one of the hospitals in the city. Apparently, my sweet husband was able to find his way with any girl based on assessing each one's personality.

I prayed to God hoping that these messages would be the worst on his list. Unfortunately, they were the least harmful ones compared to the conversation he had with his friend Sari. The first thing I saw in their WhatsApp window was a topless redhead. I froze for a moment with fear preventing me from scrolling further. I prayed again and hoped that Adi found this picture online. My wishes never came true when I read what he had written below the picture.

I'm glad I take pictures, not videos. I enjoy looking at them way more.
Prepare yourself for a bunch of hot brunettes on Monday evening.
The set will be on fire.
Hopefully, I'll get a sexy gift from one of them. The last session ended without having a happy ending. This time I'll aim for two.
Sari laughed and described him as a fucking asshole. *You're married. Leave some pussy for the rest of us. You're full, but we're the starving bastards.*

Seeing the rest of the nude pictures made me realize that my husband worked in pornography. He didn't take it as a profession only; it appeared as a lifestyle that he couldn't abandon. Cheating seemed pretty easy with all the temptations around him.

The disastrous part was that Samia and Aseel weren't good-looking, but on the other hand, the girls in the pictures shared between him and Sari were flawless. As for Yasmeen's beauty, it was too pure. My fucked-up husband had all types around him. He didn't miss anything. I wondered where I was standing in his life. Am I the sacred cup that he kept to the side to present to society while drinking from other disposable cups? Did he marry me for the sake of having children? Did he even love me? I always thought that if you love someone you wouldn't dare to hurt them or replace them with other amusements.

My body was shivering, but couldn't release tears. I kept on taking screenshots of everything and sent them to my own phone. I made sure that these screenshots were deleted from his phone to hide any evidence that could show that I held his phone. I wanted to think before I could commit any reckless action.

I didn't react when I confronted him with what I had seen. I decided to wait until Monday evening to join their big photo session based on the arrangement he had with Sari.

Waiting for him to leave the house on Monday made the wooden clock that was on our living room wall feel like it had a big stone on it preventing it from functioning as usual. At exactly six p.m., Adi stepped in to take a shower before his big night. He called me from the bathroom to reveal his big fat lie. "I have a wedding tonight and I might join Sari for a drink afterward. Don't wait for me."

I waited long enough until he left the apartment. His car was connected to a parking application that we both used. The application is used to pay for parking spaces when you park next to a blue and white sidewalk. It also has an option to see where the car that you registered is. I had to click on the 'Where is my car?' option and select the car's plate number that I had saved from before. This is the advantage of marriage: you share a house, money, and applications…to show that you're united as one. How ironic! It also helps you witness each other's mistakes and sins.

I got dressed and sat still on the chair we had in the living room, hesitating if I should go after him. I didn't want to reveal anything that could end our marriage. I had the evidence that he cheated on me with his precious models, but kept on denying the facts, refusing to believe. Thirty minutes passed while I was simply staring at the TV ahead of me. At last, I had the courage to leave that goddamn chair and call a taxi.

When I arrived at the building pointed to by the application, I saw Adi's silver car. I entered the building and walked toward the reception desk. There was a neat and pretty brunette girl sitting at the counter. I walked toward her while she was going through a bunch of folders. Without looking up at me, she reached toward a pile of papers and handed me a copy that had my husband's name on it.

ADI MAKHLOUF'S SESSION-THIRD FLOOR.

She assumed that I was one of the models without any hesitation. I headed toward the elevator when a blond model followed me to join the ride. As soon as the elevator door was closed, she stared at me from head to toe and then stared back at her phone. She didn't wait for me on her way out, and I was thankful for that. I wanted to stay unseen so I wouldn't be exposed. I wanted to know what kind of work my husband did for a living.

I stood next to a woman packing a makeup case. I was about to open my mouth when she said, "You're an hour late. We're done."

"It only takes an hour to finish such a session?" I replied.

She checked me with her eyes before answering my question.

"Apparently, you don't know Adi Makhlouf well enough. He can wrap up anything in an hour. He likes to leave some time for his own dessert."

"Where can I find him? I need to apologize for missing out on such an opportunity," I uttered with a big smile.

"He's busy now." She tried to get rid of me.

"I will wait for him. Please show me where he is and I'll be patient." I managed to control my temper.

"He's in room number 19 wrapping up some business." She exposed his location.

When I was about to leave, she grasped my hand and said, "You said that you'll wait. Don't bother him before he comes out of the room or your apology will mean shit to him."

I assured her that I wouldn't, smiling calmly.

It turned out that everyone knew my husband's business except for me. I was the dumb-ass wife that waits patiently for him at home while he fucks around with any woman with a vagina.

I broke my promise by bursting into room number 19. The first thing that I saw was his naked ass while a charming brunette was giving him a doggy-style treat. He jumped off of her once he turned his head around and saw me standing there.

The first words that came out of my mouth were, "You fuck-head monster!"

He grabbed his trousers to cover his penis as if I was foreign to him and hadn't seen his treasure before. Soon after his big jump, the girl covered herself with my husband's shirt.

I walked away from room number 19 while hearing him call my name, "Saba, wait. Saba, Habibti!"

Why would he call me a sweetheart while he was banging another sweetheart? How dare he acknowledge me as his loved one when he was fucking another woman? I think that he got this audacity after his panic attack of seeing me there. I started cursing him in my head. I recalled all the bad words that I knew and linked them all to him. I ran as fast as I could until I bumped into Sari. "Saba! What the hell are you doing here?" He shouted.

I said, with tears running down my face, "Take me out of here." He didn't hesitate to obey my request and guided me toward his car.

Once we settled in his car, he asked, "What happened and why are you here?"

"Take me home," I mouthed and then breathed in another sentence. "No, take me to your house."

"Saba, Adi wouldn't agree on such a thing," he tried to be rational.

"If you don't, someone else would. Are you willing to take me to your place or should I step out of this goddamn car?" I yelled at him.

After seeing how furious I was, he turned on the engine and drove away from the cursed crime scene.

Revenge?

I knew how rotten Sari's soul was and I wanted to take advantage of him. He led the way and opened the door of his apartment. He stood in the middle of the living room offering me something to drink. I interrupted him demanding to use his bathroom. "Please act as if you're at your own house. If you want, I can leave and return later," he offered.

"No. I want you to stay," I requested.

His bathroom was as messy and dirty as his single life. I washed my face, removed all signs of weakness that I had on it and stepped outside. I stood facing Sari who had buried his head in his phone. He felt my presence, so he asked, "Are you feeling better? Do you want to talk?"

I didn't answer. Instead, I started unbuttoning my shirt while staring at him. He didn't say a word and just watched me get undressed.

I broke the silence that was flooding the room by muttering, "Are you going to stay there? Don't you want to come closer?"

He did. He got off the sofa and came closer. He touched my face with his palm covering the right side of it. "Are you sure?" He asked.

"Continue touching me. Don't stop unless I ask you to," I ordered.

Fear overpowered him at first. He didn't dare touch anything, but my face. I removed his hand from my face and placed it on my breast. I grasped his other hand, moving it slowly from my belly toward my genitalia. My last moves unleashed his horny and aggressive side. He pushed me toward the wall that was behind us and then peeled his pants to his knees. He tried to put his cock inside me, but I pushed it out with my hand. "Not yet, big boy. You need to do me first."

"Then we need to move this to the bedroom," he mouthed in my ear. He carried my naked body and threw me on his bed. Postponing the intercourse made him work hard to earn the privilege of sticking his penis into me.

I released an orgasm filled with rage while he had his mouth playing around my clitoris. I screamed out my emotions and yelled at him to fuck me. He jumped off me to search for a condom and started running from one nightstand to the other like a maniac. I stared at him while he rambled around the room searching for a condom in one of his pants that was in his closet. This gave me a moment to regret what I had done. I realized that I had cheated on my husband with his best friend. I couldn't get dressed or escape the situation. I watched Sari put on the condom while sweat was covering his forehead. In the end, he fucked me for ten minutes while enjoying the sound of me moaning. Sari hopped off of me to lay on his back with the sound of his breathing filling the room.

He turned his head toward me and said, "You took advantage of me."

"We both benefited from this. You enjoyed it, and I got my revenge." I sighed.

"You didn't even kiss me. I didn't expect you to be such a monster in bed," he elaborated.

"I am not here to make love to you, Sari. I am here to get fucked," I boldly stated.

"And straightforward. Where did you get this courage from?" He asked.

"Your friend left me no choice," I answered.

I kept on acting as if I were strong and satisfied with what I had done, but on the inside a part of me was shattered into pieces. I left Sari lying on the bed and locked myself in his bathroom. I stepped in for a long shower, hoping that the water would cleanse my body and soul. I didn't shed a tear at that time; the image of Adi on top of that model was all I could think about. I got dressed and left Sari's house without saying goodbye.

In my Eastern society, if women cheat on their husbands, their husbands have the right to kill them to restore their stolen honor and show that they are manly enough to punish their wives. If the case was reversed and a man cheated on his wife, everyone expects the woman to see it as a fling that she should overlook in order to move on and fix their broken relationship. This society sees it as the woman's fault in this scenario; she couldn't satisfy her husband and he had to look for other options outside his own house. My monstrous society considers it as a fair and balanced equation. Eastern women are blinded by this theory that was created by men, judging and oppressing other women based on it.

Let me retell the true events of what happened at Sari's apartment. I stepped out of Sari's bathroom and stood in the middle of the living room. Sari's face was indeed buried in his phone. He felt my presence so he asked, "Are you feeling better? Do you want to talk?"

I imagined the whole scenario of cheating on my husband and how it would make me feel. I knew that the satisfaction would last for only a few minutes. I knew that I would never forgive myself for cheating on myself before cheating on Adi. The end result was that I headed to the door and abandoned what would've damaged my soul. I took a taxi and headed to my parents' house. A whole array of emotions overwhelmed me. On the one hand, I wished I had fucked his handsome best friend, but on the other hand, I felt ashamed of myself for even thinking about that and blamed Adi for dragging me down the road with him.

I knocked on the door several times until my mother opened the door for me. "Saba! Is everything ok?" She asked when she saw me standing opposite her. She was able to tell this wasn't a normal visit.

"I want to stay the night here," I answered.

"What's wrong?" She asked again.

"I just need some rest and want to spend the night here," I said in a calm voice.

She couldn't let it go. "Is it Adi? What did he do?"

I couldn't answer calmly this time. "For the love of God, leave me the hell alone! I just need to sleep in my fucking bed!"

She didn't dare ask more questions after I yelled at her. She was the last person on earth that I could trust with such problems.

I laid my head on my old pillow and turned on my phone to find 50 WhatsApp messages from my beloved Adi begging me to come back home. My phone started ringing. Apparently, he had been calling me since I had left that building.

Saba, baby please answer my calls.

Saba, I know you cannot forgive me for what you saw and you have the entire right not to.

My mom opened the door to check on me, but I couldn't give her any of my attention. I got my headphones out of my purse, turned the lights off, and played some music to separate me from the cruel outside world. I played a song by Sam Smith called *Dancing with a Stranger*. I wished that the lyrics of the song matched my story. Foolishly, I didn't want to dance with anyone, but Adi.

I played the song over and over again until I fell asleep.

The sunbeam breaking through the window forced me to open my eyes. I remembered the previous night. I remembered the horrible act that I was about to make. I recalled every detail and every move I had made after I realized that I had married a big, fat scumbag who wouldn't turn down any offer of sex dangling before him. My throat was painfully sour from all the disappointment that I had. I wrapped my arms around my legs and released the river of tears that came all the way from my broken heart.

My youngest sister Haya interrupted my mourning when she asked me to join them for breakfast. I wiped my tears away and asked, "Why aren't you at school?"

"We're off. It's Sunday."

I couldn't tell what day it was. The trauma that stormed through me made me forget that it was my day off as well. I was relieved that I didn't tank my job by not showing up to my classes. Haya moved on and said, "A face like yours shouldn't be sad or upset. You're the prettiest and smartest of us. Please, cheer up! If Adi is the one to blame, I can kick his ass for you."

I laughed out of courtesy to assure my eleven-year-old sister that nothing was wrong even though my world was collapsing all around me.

The smell of fried eggs made its way to my nose and made me nauseous. The more I inched closer to it, the more it made me want to throw up. At last, the mission was accomplished. I vomited yellowish saliva in the bathroom sink which almost made me choke. I started yelling, "How can someone vomit if the fucking stomach is empty!" My mother answered the call by laughing and staring at me. I was provoked, seeing that she found my misery amusing to her. "Why are you laughing and smiling? I don't feel well."

"It's because you're pregnant, my dear," she proclaimed.

A Shoulder to Lean On

A swirl of commands.

A storm of criticism.

Some seek doing what they don't dare to do vicariously through you.

Love hides in times of pressure. Eyes get blinded with anxiety.

Your beloved ones turn into fading memories while they're still with you in person.

A cracking wall starts collapsing between two places, turning them into one.

Keeping what is left of you becomes the biggest challenge in times of transition.

The shoulder that you lean on to find comfort becomes the one that hurts your thoughts.

My Cursed Fetus

I started vomiting following every meal, and if I didn't, I felt that I was about to throw up again. I thought that this was happening because of my mental and miserable situation. My bad fortune didn't let me think of the possibility of being pregnant. I didn't feel that it was right to bring a baby into our lives at this time.

I couldn't accept this idea and prayed that it was just a cold that would eventually go away. I got dressed and headed to the medical center. The receptionist gave me a number and asked me to go to room number 10 to see the physician. The chair I sat in shook with me, and my head started boiling with malicious thoughts. I waited for the patient to finish his checkup before I went in and handed the doctor my medical card which had all of my medical information. He swiped it into the machine attached to his computer and asked, "How can I help you, Ms. Makhlouf?"

"I want to do a pregnancy test, please," I replied.

He typed in a report, printed it out, and handed it to me. "Please give it to the nurse at the emergency room, and he will take your blood sample. If the result is positive, please get an appointment through the reception to see the gynecologist."

I did as he ordered. Once the nurse took the blood sample, he asked me to wait in the waiting room for the result. "Today is your lucky day. We don't have many patients so you won't have to wait too long for the result," he assured me. The sort of day I was having depended on the result, and I hoped that luck would be my ally.

I leaned my head against the wall behind me and closed my eyes. I wished to undo all that had happened the night before. I wished to erase from my memory what I had seen the other night. My thoughts were disturbed by the nurse when he said, "Congratulations! You're pregnant." He was thrilled to hand me the paper that had a circle around the word 'POSITIVE'. I took the paper and rushed to my father's car. I started hitting my head against the steering wheel begging God to undo this. I didn't deserve this baby, and neither did Adi. I started thinking that I was going to commit adultery with a growing fetus inside me. He would've been the accomplice in the sin I had almost committed.

I walked into my parents' house to find Adi waiting for me in the living room. "Your mother says that you have good news," he uttered in my mother's presence. I ignored him and walked into my room. I heard my mother's whispers asking him to follow me. He entered the room to find me lying on the bed with my body facing the wall next to the bed. He sat next to me and called my name.

"Get the fuck out! You're the last person on earth I want to see right now," I mouthed with anger.

"Just look at me, please!" he asked.

I rolled myself to the other side of the bed and held myself up to yell at him. "How dare you show up here! Do you want me to go outside and tell my parents what you did? You should leave if you want to avoid the scandal that I am about to make."

"Please don't yell. Let's talk about this at home," he whispered.

"You son of a bitch," I yelled again.

"I am a son of a bitch. You have all the right to call me any name you want. Please get all of your rage out, and I promise that I'll do anything you want," he said, trying to calm me down.

"I want you to get the fuck out of here and leave me the hell alone or I will go out and tell my parents everything," I threatened.

"I love you, Saba. I swear to God that I do! I wish I could go back in time and undo what I did." He tried to win my sympathy.

"You don't love me, and I doubt that you ever did. I'm sure that if I didn't walk in on you fucking her, you would've repeated it over and over again. I will do the same thing to you, Adi. I am going to cheat on you. Just wait for it." I made a new threat.

He reached for my hand and begged me not to say that. "I know you better than I know myself. You wouldn't do it. You have more morals than I do."

I wanted to hurt him and lie to his face. "I already did. I cheated on you yesterday. I slept with another man."

He refused to believe me and denied it. "I know you didn't. I wouldn't believe it even if I had seen it with my own eyes."

"But I did. I slept with someone else," I repeated.

He ignored my lie. He refused to consider it as a fact. He thought of it as my way of getting back at him.

"Please, sweetheart! Come back home. I promise I'll give you all the space you need. Please don't leave me alone for another night. You know I can't live without you," he begged.

I had no energy to scold him or go through this with him again. I just needed to sleep in order to forget about reality for a while. I ignored his last words, turned my body toward the wall again, and closed my eyes. He placed his hand on my shoulder, forcing me to whisper with irritation, "Leave me alone. I just want to sleep without having your breath or your body near me."

Ten days have passed since that night. Whenever I received a phone call or a text message from him, I had to swipe it aside so it would disappear out of my sight.

I waited for an hour for my turn at the gynecologist's clinic. Married couples kept on entering and leaving that room while I was waiting there alone with my fetus. I stared at the ceiling to avoid the sympathetic looks I got from the couples that were around me. On that day, my heart started racing when I saw my fetus and heard its heartbeat. I was two months pregnant with an actual human being that was conceived by Adi and me.

I left the clinic to have a fight with myself. A part of me wanted to be selfish and choose the easiest solution of killing this innocent creature. Another part of me was merciful and dying for this baby to grow inside me so I could meet him/her. Two parts within me thought about this creature as both a human being and a lifeless object at the same time. I lost my sense of direction when I found myself roaming around in the market of the old city of Jerusalem. Merchants were screaming out of the top of their lungs while advertising their goods; women were bargaining to get lower prices for fruits; young girls were shopping for clothes; and young boys were annoying people walking through the market with their bicycles, I was stopped by a tiny little dress that was on display at a children's clothing shop. I walked into the store and bought the fluffy pink dress.

I didn't know what the baby's gender was, but once I bought the dress, I decided to keep him\her. I placed my hand on my belly and whispered, "I will protect you with all my strength, and if you turn out to be a boy, I promise that I'll buy you something more manly. I got your back, my innocent and beautiful creature!"

The decision I made forced me to surrender and accept Adi's apology. I returned to our house on my own volition. I didn't tell him that I was coming back. The house was a complete mess and needed cleaning. I got my cleaning kit out and started dusting, washing, and vacuuming. I wanted to cook a decent meal, but there was nothing edible in the fridge and I was in no condition to smell any type of food. Seeing or smelling meat made me feel sick.

I heard the clank of Adi's keys unlocking the door; I closed my eyes and pretended to be asleep because I couldn't stand to see his face. He walked slowly toward the bedroom to find me there. I thought that he wouldn't disturb me, but he was thrilled to see me lying there with clean bed sheets beneath me. He lay down next to me and whispered in my ear, "Everything became more shiny when you came back home. I am nothing without you and I won't accept living a life without you in it." He started kissing me on my shoulder and tried to push his private parts into my behind with his clothes on. I turned myself toward him and asked him to let me rest.

"I still need time to overcome what we've been through. Please don't expect to get anything from me."

He didn't accept my request and moved on to say, "You don't have to make any effort; I'll do everything. All you have to do is lie down."

I refused what he was asking for, got up, and walked away to sit on a chair that was facing the bed. "If I am back, it doesn't mean that everything will be the same as before. I need time and you need to respect that. If we want our marriage to work, we need to start taking each other's feelings into consideration so we can build a healthy family together," I said firmly.

"I'll do whatever it takes to regain your trust. You're my family!" He knew the exact words he needed to say to fool me.

I didn't reply to his statement, so he asked, "What changed your mind? Why did you come back?"

"We're having a baby. You should respect the family we're about to have together, Adi."

My sentence made him jump out of bed and repeat the same question three times in a row. "You're pregnant?"

Confirming that I was pregnant had a magical effect on him. He started jumping and screaming with joy until he made his way toward my belly to speak to our future child, "Baba, I am here! Can you hear me? I am sorry for upsetting you and your Mama." He shifted himself up next to my face and kissed me on the forehead announcing that he'd take good care of me and the baby, and my fragile self, believed him. For a moment, it seemed as if nothing had happened, and that all of the mistakes he had made were a figment of our imagination.

My mother called me the next day to tell me that I did the right thing by going back to my husband. She started mumbling that once a woman gets married, she should accept all of the circumstances of her marriage. She mentioned that a woman should suck it up and accept her destiny so she won't gain the title of a divorced woman. She moved on to describe divorced women as easy objects since the way to their vagina becomes open and easy to get into.

The conversation ended with a fight because I didn't agree with what she was saying. Her most remarkable sentence was: *Your Western ideas won't help you or add to your life. You should have your feet glued to the ground and accept our reality. Once a woman is married, she should give up her own needs to fulfill the needs of her husband and children.* It was funny hearing those words from her since she neither treated my father nor her own children well. Her idea of motherhood was all about keeping the house clean and having food on the table at the end of the day. She neglected herself and us at the same time, which meant there was no winning side in this case. This is what her mother had taught her, and she wanted to pass down these words of 'wisdom' to keep the legacy alive. I tried to accept that I could not change her way of thinking because she had never known any other reality.

Two days passed before Sari heard the good news about me and Adi getting back together. I was taking a shower when I heard Adi welcoming him in. Adi came running toward the bathroom to ask if I had proper clothes to put on. I asked him to bring me a pair of jeans and a T-shirt to wear. He sneaked the clothes into the bathroom while Sari was waiting to witness my big appearance. I wanted to hide in the bedroom because I was afraid that Sari had figured out what my true intentions were when I went to his house the other day. For some reason, I felt he was able to read my thoughts.

I left the bathroom wearing the clothes Adi had brought me and shame. I headed toward the living room to meet our precious guest. I welcomed him and asked him if he'd like to drink coffee. Adi turned to answer on Sari's behalf, saying, "If you let him choose, he would drink anything that is the opposite of coffee."

Sari started to laugh nervously while trying to keep up with Adi. "Coffee is fine. I still have the rest of the night to dull its effect."

I poured the coffee into small cups that I placed on the middle table. Adi offered to hand Sari and himself their cups so I could rest and do nothing since the special treatment had already started. "I'll leave you two alone and get some rest," I uttered. In return, Adi wrapped his arm around my shoulder to stop me from leaving the room so he could announce the news of my pregnancy. "You need to congratulate us, brother. We're expecting a baby soon!"

Sari choked on the sip of coffee he had taken, and the cup of coffee fell on the floor as it slipped out of his hand. I wanted to rush to the kitchen to bring something to wipe away the mess he had made but was stopped again by Adi. "I got this, dear. Stay rested."

I tried to avoid eye contact with Sari. But Sari's eyes were all over me. "Why did you flee from my apartment the other day? I couldn't understand why you stood there debating whether to come closer or not before you left," he whispered so Adi wouldn't hear him.

He stopped for a second waiting to get a reaction or an answer when he realized that he would get neither.

He dared to declare what he wished would've happened. "Call me sick, but part of me wanted you to come closer."

"You are sick if you're trying to get to a dark place with what you are saying," I finally said.

I stood up and gave out my final statement with a forced smile on my face that showed how disgusted I was with him. "Remember that I am carrying your friend's baby. You will be his favorite uncle soon, brother."

I was mad at myself more than I was mad at him. I dragged myself into the filthy circle of Sari's and Adi's world. I saved myself from disaster when I ran away from Sari's apartment that day.

Tahseen

For too long, I was reminded of how I had married into a society with which I shared nothing in common. It was an arranged marriage after all that didn't allow me an opportunity to know what I was marrying into. I just found myself living in the same house with that very society, according to the rules and standards that were set by him/it. The first idea I had about it was when I was young and was told that I should limit displaying too much of my body as it wasn't accepted by the man of the house. Rather, I should please and cherish him for the rest of my life. If I, in any way, violated the rules of my society, I would be damned by everyone around me and I would lose my good reputation. My mother, aunts, neighbors, and all the females around me frightened me out of doing anything that could smudge my reputation.

You need to behave well.

Your voice shouldn't be loud in the streets and don't you dare laugh out loud in public.

Wear layers of clothes so that when your blouse pulls up by mistake, your back won't be shown.

Cover the line of your breasts or they'll say you're a whore.

Don't speak to boys. They'll brag about it in front of their friends and your reputation will be ruined and you'll never get married.

Don't go out on dates. If your father, brother, neighbor, or someone who knows you sees you, then you'll be punished and maybe beaten to death.

You're not allowed to kiss except when you're married.

Good girls never stay out late. They're home before darkness pervades the sky.

If your mother-in-law says something offensive, don't you dare answer her or say something against her word.

Your husband should always find a meal on the table when he enters the house.

Your house should be always clean or they'll speak badly about you.

Your husband comes first and everyone else comes last. If he forbids you to do something, you'll need to obey him.

Pleasing your husband sexually is an important task. Otherwise, he'll start playing around outside the house.

If your husband gets angry and starts swearing at you, you should stay silent until he gets calm.

Divorce is not an option. Just suck it in and swallow the offense so you can give your kids a healthy life.

Your kids come after your husband and your happiness last.

Basically, you're a slave to your husband for the rest of your life.

What's hard to understand? We know what's best for you.

Disobeying the traditions and the commands of my husband/society was not an option. When you try to break out of the concrete that was poured on you throughout the years, you will find yourself trapped under layers. Each layer you break will make you lose certain privileges that are only meant to be given to good and decent girls.

We found out the gender of our baby during our visit to the doctor's clinic. The doctor rubbed my belly with a cold gel and started moving the ultrasound so we could see the baby on the big screen that was ahead of us. The baby was full of energy and was swimming inside of me. Adi jumped and started shouting, "Look at his thingy. It's a boy. Am I right, doctor?"

The doctor confirmed by nodding her head and smiling.

He couldn't wait to call his parents and pass them the good news, so he dialed his father's number when we got into the car. "We're having a boy. Tahseen is on his way to join the family."

I was happy to find out the gender of the baby, but it dismayed me that my baby boy would be given an ugly name after an ugly-hearted man. Adi was attached to his family's tradition and had always believed that his firstborn child should be named after his father since he was the eldest male among his siblings. He didn't care that the name was old-fashioned and that his baby would hate it.

I stayed silent regarding the fact that I hated the name until I reached my eighth month of pregnancy. We were having dinner, and I had the courage to tell him that I couldn't stand the name Tahseen. He stroked his hands on the table and shouted, "People knew me as the father of Tahseen all my life. My son will be named Tahseen after my father whether you like it or not."

No matter how educated and open-minded a man is within the society I was raised in, they'll never dare to cross the line when it comes to following traditions.

The Miracle of Birth
April 2018

Inducing labor was all I was thinking about when I reached my 41st week. I started walking for an hour a day, I tried drinking castor oil, and I had sex with my husband, and followed any mythical way that people around me suggested.

I woke up one morning to find a gluey liquid on my underwear. My desperation made me think that my water broke so I called Adi to tell him that I was taking a taxi to the hospital. He gave a cold explanation because he didn't witness me scream like he saw in the movies. "I think you'll know if your water broke. It's not something you suspect, my dear."

"I am overdue and will finish my tenth month of pregnancy soon. Something must be wrong. I am going to the hospital," I insisted.

I didn't wait for his approval or for him to rush home to take me to the hospital. I got out of the taxi and walked toward the hospital's main entrance. "I think my water broke, but I am not sure," I told the nurse who was standing in the emergency room. She guided me to the emergency section that was designed for pregnant women and helped me get on one of the beds. She asked for my ID and informed me about some papers that I needed to fill out before the arrival of the doctor. I handed her my ID, and in return, she got back with a plastic bracelet that had my name and ID printed on it.

Adi walked into the emergency room to find a monitor wrapped around my belly. "They're monitoring the heartbeat of the baby," I explained to him the situation I was in. He grabbed the chair next to my bed and moved it closer to me.

He sat on the chair, leaned toward my hand, and kissed it. "Are you in pain, my love?"

"I am not feeling anything other than the baby kicking. I can't stand staying pregnant for another day. I want to see my baby," I muttered.

"We're almost there. Tahseen will lighten up our world soon," he tried to comfort me.

Our conversation was interrupted by a petite doctor trying to assure me, with a smile on his face that everything was going to be ok. It took me a while to recognize the doctors at the hospital since I thought they were supposed to be dressed in white. I was shocked to know that the doctors in this section were all dressed in green while the midwives were dressed in purple.

The petite doctor asked Adi to leave the room so he could do an internal examination to determine the cervix dilation and to track if I was ready to give birth. "Please take off your pants and underwear and cover yourself with the bedspread that is beneath you," he asked politely.

"I think my water broke," I said.

"We'll check on that in a bit in the other room. What I am about to do is going to hurt if you don't relax your body. Please relax and I'll try to be gentle so it won't hurt," he explained.

I did as he asked, except for the relaxing part. That was the first time that someone other than my husband would put his fingers inside me. I couldn't let go of how annoying the idea was. As a result, I started moaning out of pain.

"Your cervix is not open enough, the dilation is only one and a half," he emphasized.

"Do you mean I am not ready to give birth?" I asked.

"We'll check on the water first and then we'll decide what to do. However, if your water didn't break, then we'll have two options: either you go home and wait for another week and see if you'll experience contractions, or we start the dilation now and you stay here to give birth to your lovely baby," he explained.

"Does it hurt? How will you induce it?" I asked.

"I'll have to put my fingers in again and help start the dilation," he responded.

"How long will this take, I mean with your fingers inside me?" I asked again.

"Ten seconds only. It will hurt, but it'll start the process of labor," he said while trying to make it sound harmless.

I agreed to the second option, thinking that a pain that lasts for ten seconds only is better than hanging on for another week.

Adi kept on going out for a smoke every 15 minutes, and if it wasn't for a smoke, it would be to get a cup of coffee. His mother stayed next to me more than he did, and my own mother joined the party afterward.

The light curtains that were between me and the women next to me forced me to be familiar with their lives and helped me get a glimpse into the way they were treated by their husbands and families. One of those women had five people next to her bed. She had her father, father-in-law, two sisters, and her mother. Her father-in-law kept on discussing religious matters and started lecturing the women around him about the importance of the Hijab (headscarf). He shifted his lectures to a whole political stream. The theories he had were all based on gossip, Facebook videos, and what his male neighbors discussed in front of him. He had no accurate source of what he was saying, yet the females around him seemed to agree with whatever he said.

Another Israeli woman next to me seemed to be comfortable with her situation since this was her sixth baby. She video-chatted with her five other children to check on them, assuring them that she'll be back home soon with their baby brother, Yaron.

The diversity in the hospital was amusing—I saw Arab women, Israeli women, Orthodox Jews, Muslims, and Christians and there was even an Indian lady who entered the room with water all over her skirt. Seeing that Indian woman made me realize that I was stupid to think that my water had broken earlier that day. This fact was confirmed by the doctor as well when he tested for it by squeezing a tool inside of me that looked like a stick at first but then popped open like an umbrella inside my vagina.

I hated the fact that I couldn't erase the scene of giving birth to my first child out of my head. It was horrible. My mother and mother-in-law were on their phones all the time passing the news to everyone in the family. Everyone we knew was updated on every step I made in the hospital. I felt that everyone I knew was checking on me out of custom and tradition. I didn't feel loved or cared for by anyone in the room with me, except for the midwife and the doctor.

I didn't question taking the epidural. It was a huge help until I started feeling some pain. I was instructed to press the button that was hanging from a wire whenever I felt that the epidural effect was about to go away. I kept pressing it, but the pain didn't go away so I called the midwife again to tell her that something was wrong. She started screaming in Hebrew that I shouldn't have pressed the button because the baby's head was starting to come out.

The battle of bringing the baby out to life began while I was being scolded by my husband for doing it wrong. "Push as if you're going to the bathroom," Adi ordered.

"I am. This is how I go to the bathroom!" I yelled back at him.

He kept on ordering me to do something that I was already trying to do, but I was held back because of my lack of experience. Instead of pushing the baby out, I pushed him back in because I couldn't feel anything starting from my waist to my last toe. "Let's take a break, and we'll get back to you soon when you're ready again," the doctor uttered.

I rested my head on the pillow behind me to prepare myself for the next round of battle. My break lasted for less than 15 minutes before they came back to check on me.

Adi began to yell at me again as if I was not pushing the baby out on purpose. I couldn't handle the pressure that he was putting me under so I looked back at him with sweat covering my forehead and yelled, "If you'll yell at me, you better get out." His temper cooled down after he realized he was making things worse.

Another doctor in green was called for help while the midwife and the first doctor tried to observe the baby's progress as it tried to crawl out of my body. The doctor, who had spent only ten seconds in the room with me, noticed that Adi was standing next to my legs so as to witness the birth of his child while I was left alone at the other end of the bed. The doctor in green stood next to me, held my hand, and started asking me to breathe. He had one hand squeezed into mine and another hand trying to squeeze the baby out of my body by messaging my belly in a way to push him out. For a brief moment, I was shocked that this complete stranger, one who had a different religion than mine, showed me more mercy than my own husband.

The rest of my stay at the hospital wasn't pleasant either. Whenever I turned my head around to look for Adi through the crowd, I couldn't find him. Even during nighttime, it was only me and the baby with no one to guide us through this new journey or offer any comfort. I was alone with my baby in a dark room, scared and surrounded by women who seemed to know better. I was just an ignorant woman, and I felt that my hands were paralyzed because I didn't know how to change a diaper or breastfeed my child.

The first night was the hardest. It was my first stop with my child, all alone in this world that was full of adventures yet cruel.

Motherhood

My mother once told me that my siblings and I were not her children. She said that we held a different family name than hers; therefore, we belonged to my dad and his family. Her exact words were *Even though I gave birth to you, you're not mine and you will never be. Whatever you do will be in the name of your family, not my name.*

She had always treated us as enemies because we were able to love my father's family.

She was able to do the same with my son. She refused to take care of him and didn't care to see him. She asked my father to pass me a message. "He's not Saba's son. He's the son of the Makhlouf family. They'll take him away from here eventually. Tell Saba not to put so much effort into this kid."

She thought that she could deprive me of my own child like she did. She thought I was cold-hearted like she was, and that I could treat my own son as a stranger. Some humans don't deserve to have the privilege of being called 'mothers' and mine never acted as one.

I grew up witnessing my mother spread poison wherever she went. The friends she used to get along with were like her. They had a master's degree in gossip and specialized in finding ways to wreck homes with their wagging tongues. They also shared similar beliefs thinking that people were envying them for their lives. They would lie and say that they were miserable so no one would give them the evil eye.

We had a neighbor who was one of my mother's best friends; she used to tell us bad stories about her husband. She would tell us that he was cheap, that he cheated on her, that he didn't bring food to the house, and that he was relying on her financially. Yet, I witnessed the opposite as, on several occasions, I saw him holding bags filled with groceries while, at other times, I used to see his kids playing with all sorts of expensive toys that were bought by him. This 'oppressed' woman used to complain about her in-laws as well. However, whenever they visited her, she would kiss them on both cheeks and prepare the finest dishes, all with a smile that reached the sky from happiness as if the royal family had visited her.

Her malicious accusations, which were based on jealousy, reached me when she once told my mother that her husband fancies me, and she told her to warn me about him. My mother didn't defend me or try to shut her up. Instead, she came running to warn me as her best friend had demanded. My reply to her warning was full of disappointment. "And you didn't say a word? You didn't even tell her to shut the fuck up for saying such nonsense? You think I'll fast and never have men in my life and then break my fasting with her bastard husband?"

Eventually, my mother's poison seeped into my own house. It happened through stages—she didn't pour it all down my glass at once. She relished squeezing my soul in her hand and witnessing the last broken piece of it fall down; she enjoyed the act of breaking me, hoping that I would crawl back to her and to my vicious husband begging for mercy. She thought she was doing me a favor by breaking me so I wouldn't be able to hold my head high while staying under her control forever.

The first stage of her mission started three days after I gave birth to my son. She left the house after she had had a big fight with my father and siblings. The heartbreaking part was that my grandmother was there trying to calm her down, begging her to stay home. "Your daughter just gave birth. She needs you by her side now more than ever! Wash your face and calm down—we'll find a solution to whatever this is about."

My mother's storm was shooting with flames; she didn't think about anyone, but herself at that moment, which was the case most of the time. "They have no respect for me in this house. I cannot accept being treated like a doormat! My brother is waiting for me outside in his car, and my family will take care of me now," she arrogantly shouted.

The mental damage started when I stepped into the house with my infant. I knew about their big fight from Adi even though he was away on a work trip. My mother told my husband about their problems so as to seek his attention and be able to enjoy playing the victim's role for her new audience. When I asked her why she told Adi about it, she answered me saying, "I wanted him to take extra care of you through these rough times." She thought that my absent husband would take care of me while she continued her attempt to slowly kill me.

The global crisis of my mother's leaving the house was on everyone's mind, and it was the only thing that was spoken about at my house. My father would spend the night over, complaining about my mother's behavior while narrating anecdotes about what a bad wife and mother she was. On the other hand, my mother would spend her days hovering around me, crying and talking about her miserable life and all the torture she had been through throughout her years of marriage. I was lost between them and between maintaining my own sanity, which I needed to be able to take care of the new human being in my hands.

Adi came back from his trip hoping he could fix everything and be the hero of the day. He became too involved and enjoyed listening to all of my family's dirty secrets. Seeing how vulnerable I was made him spread his wings like a peacock and think he could walk all over me without feeling any kind of guilt. I tried to cut Adi out by begging my mother to keep the details of their private life to herself, telling her that it was affecting my own family. Her most outrageous sentences throughout the crisis were:

He's my son-in-law; he should check on me all the time. Why didn't he call me?

I cannot break my brothers' word and go back to your father. He should learn his lesson, and your siblings should learn how to behave around their mother.

I cannot take the humiliation. My dignity is above everything.

I am wrecked between my own family and my brothers. If you were me, what would you do?

I want a divorce. Enough is enough.

My sister called me and explained how tough it would be to live as a divorced lady in this society after all of these years. Imagine being a divorced 51-year-old woman! I want to go back to your father. How can I make this happen?

All of these drama and therapy sessions were taking place at my house while my baby cried the whole time. All of these sessions created a state of discomfort for my poor child. I tried to breastfeed him, but he refused my milk.

I tried to pump my milk into a bottle, but he spit it out as soon as it reached his mouth. I couldn't maintain a good mental state to help me focus on my baby while relatives from my father's and mother's sides would only discuss my parents' problems when they came to visit me.

On one rainy day, Adi invited my mother over for dinner at our house by saying that he wanted to get her mind off of her issues. Adi dropped her over at our house and then left to deal with one of his photography sessions. He called his mother to join us and keep us company. For some reason, to my good fortune, his mother couldn't join us that day.

My mother's face was a mix of red and anger. I could sense that something was wrong. I couldn't focus on interpreting her facial expressions, or ask what was wrong. Two days had passed without being able to get two hours of continuous sleep so I asked in an exhausting voice, "Can you please watch him? I just need to close my eyes for half an hour." I asked for some rest, and she temporarily yielded to me. Twenty-eight minutes later, Tahseen's crying forced my eyes open. I took him out of her arms and tried to calm him down.

The ticking bomb inside my mother's face blew right at me. "You don't care about your mother! You're just like your sister—you're a selfish daughter! You won't even step up to help me or care about what will happen to me."

My eyes widened as I screamed back at her. "I haven't slept in two days, and my baby won't shut up. He keeps crying! He doesn't even want my own milk, and you're accusing me of being one of the reasons behind your misery!? What did I do to you?"

"You're not helping, and you don't care about your own mother," she insisted on blaming me.

"Please keep your voice down; my mother-in-law will be here soon. Please don't embarrass me," I begged.

My request only made her shout and scream at me even more. She started praying to God to take my life and my siblings' lives away. In the end, she took her stuff and headed to the door to leave.

I put my baby on the bed despite his crying and followed her. "Please wait! I'll drive you once Adi gets back to watch the baby. It's getting dark outside, how will you go back? Mom, I am begging you! Please don't leave like this!"

She refused to listen to me and left the house crying and cursing the day she gave birth to us. She probably hoped she'd meet my mother-in-law going down the stairs, but her wishes came to naught and I was saved from being humiliated once again in front of Adi's family.

A Mistake That Led to Our Existence

My father enjoyed telling the story of how he had married my mother. It drove my mother crazy every time he did it in the presence of new friends or family members. She would roll her eyes at him and shout at him with irritation. "Mousa, stop it. No one wants to hear the story. You're making it sound like you were forced to marry me. Everyone knows that this is not true."

He would laugh and continue narrating the events that led to their marriage, ignoring her warnings not to proceed.

The last time I heard him tell the story was when I became engaged to Adi. We were all sitting around the dining table when my father offered to tell Adi the amusing story of how he met his wife Suad.

We lived in a small village in East Jerusalem where everyone knew each other. The girls were hidden away most of the time inside their homes, and the boys would take a glimpse of them whenever they were on their way to school or going out with their families. Their love stories were all about eye contact and, if they were lucky enough, they would exchange letters. The most courageous thing that some lovers did was to meet in the fields, hiding under trees to exchange conversations or even steal a kiss. Arranged marriages were all they knew, and even if they shared a love story, they would pretend that they had never met so their families would think it was an arranged marriage as well.

The story of my parents took a different route; one small mistake ruined one of my father's dreams. Behind all the laughing and joking I was able to sense the disappointment he still had felt.

I liked a girl that used to live close to our neighborhood. I told my mother about her and asked her to tell my dad that I wanted to marry her. My mother called them after she got my father's approval.

My uncle's wife accompanied my mother to see the girl I liked and to meet the female members of her family before we'd all go to ask for her hand.

My mother was sneaky. She went to their house at 7:00 a.m. so she could see the girl without makeup to evaluate her natural looks.

The big event took place when my father, mother, and I paid them a visit so we could make things official and ask for her hand in marriage, according to our traditions and customs. My mother passed the front door of the girl's house and walked toward the door of my dream girl's neighbors. I thought that I had been mistaken and that my mother knew where the girl actually lived. I trusted my mother to guide us toward the correct house.

The bride's older brother and mother sat with us while we waited for the bride to make an appearance. At last, she walked in carrying a tray with cups of coffee on it and...BOOM! The big surprise exploded on my face. It wasn't the girl I had my eyes on. It was your mother!

I whispered in my mother's ear, "This is not the girl I told you about." She couldn't hear me with all the noise around us while trying to focus on the conversation my father was having with the bride's family.

I whispered again to both my parents as soon as we got out of the house, "That's not her. She's not the one I told you about. I think the one I want lives next door."

My father gave me an angry look with smoke coming out of his ears. "You son of a bitch! We asked for this one's hand, and she seemed like a polite girl. We need to uphold what we just did and wait for their answer. Let's hope that they'll say no if you're saying you don't want to marry her."

My mother and I followed his steps toward the main street and watched him mumble to himself with anger. "He wants to marry a bitch. The one we saw seemed nice and well-raised. The son of a bitch wants to embarrass me!"

My father's prayers weren't answered. They said yes.

If they had never made this mistake, and if they hadn't knocked on the wrong door, I would've been a ghost that never existed. Because of this mistake, my siblings and I were assigned to this life. Their destiny wrote our story along with theirs.

Smashed

It had been two weeks since we had had our big argument. We fought over the deleted messages he had on his Facebook Messenger. The only thing he focused on was the following question: "How did you know we had a conversation going on? You're such a sneaky woman." He thought that he would get his way out of trouble if he laughed at the matter and acted as if he didn't care. I didn't let go of this because of all the cheating he had done in the past.

"How come you're so comfortable with mistreating me?" I questioned.

"You're making a big deal out of nothing," he coldly answered.

"It's not nothing. Something fishy is going on here. If you won't tell me the truth, I'll reach out to your beloved friend and ask her myself," I threatened.

"Don't you dare disrespect me in front of her. I told you, she's just a co-worker and we're working on something together," he answered.

"If it's just work, why did you delete the messages?" I wondered aloud, with anger written all over my face.

"How did you even know that we had a conversation?" he dared to ask.

"She's not added to your friends list, but you're connected on Messenger. It means you had a conversation and that's how you got connected. It doesn't take a technology genius to figure this out," I shot back at him from across the room.

"I'm going to change my phone's password. You've left me no other choice," he replied with his head buried in his phone.

"If you do that, I'll make you regret it for the rest of your life," I threatened again.

"You're crossing the line, Saba. Watch yourself!" He stopped looking at his phone and faced me. I was able to provoke him.

"You started it. You used to cheat on me all the time and thought that I wouldn't reveal it. How can I trust you again?" I lost my confidence and turned down my tone.

"I cannot tolerate your craziness anymore. I'm leaving the house," he ended the argument by running away.

Leaving the house didn't stop me from chasing him with a phone call. I couldn't put out the fire burning inside my head and body. I started the call by saying, "You're going to block this girl and never speak to her again."

He refused my demand, forcing me to threaten him one more time. "I'll write her and ask her to tell me about all of the conversations you two have had."

He couldn't ignore my threats and that made him scream at me. "You want to disrespect me in front of my coworkers? I'll destroy you if you contact her! I'll fucking break you, you hear me?"

"Don't you talk to me like this! You're the one who's screwing around! You're already dishonoring me by speaking to and fucking other women!" I yelled back at him with tears running down my eyes.

"Listen, you crabby woman, if you do anything I don't like, consider yourself divorced! I'll throw you out on the street and you'll never see your dear baby ever again!" He unleashed the real monster that had been lurking inside of him all along.

"Who the fuck do you think you are to talk to me like this?" He ignored my shouting and hung up on me, leaving my body in shivers.

We ignored each other's existence for two weeks following this argument. Anger grew inside our guts, and we both couldn't stand the sight of each other. When he'd step into bed, we'd both make sure to stick to each opposite edge.

At exactly 6:23 p.m., I received a phone call from my father telling me that my sister had broken her hip after falling from a great height. "Her foot slipped while playing with water balloons outside the house with your cousin."

I prepared the baby's bag to join my family at the hospital despite my father's request for me to stay home with my son.

I had to put the war I had with Adi on hold and ask for the car keys.

"Why do you need the car?" He asked while washing his face in the bathroom sink.

"My sister is at the hospital." I stood in the doorway, facing him.

"I'll come with you," he said.

"I don't want you to be around me and act as if nothing is wrong between us. I can't put up appearances this time," I said with my hands moving in circles.

"I'm not pleased with your company either, but I want to be there for your sister," the noble Adi declared.

"She's my sister, and my presence will be good enough for her. She doesn't need to see you." My mean self fought back.

He was provoked enough to throw the towel in his hand on the floor. The veins on his forehead bulged as anger started coursing through his body. He kept his body in control though, except for his tongue and eyes. He inched two steps closer to me and mouthed, "You know what? Two weeks have passed by and I just feel like squeezing your head and bashing it into the wall!"

I unleashed the secret weapon that could wound any Eastern man deep inside and dared to say the following forbidden words. "And you consider yourself a man? You're nothing close to being a man."

I dropped the bomb and left him to digest what he had just heard. I foolishly thought he would ignore what I had just said and went to check on the baby to see if his diaper needed changing. As my hands reached the middle of the bed to grab my baby, I felt him aggressively grabbing me by the arm to throw me away from the bed. "Do you know what a man is, you fucking bitch? I am going to show you what a man is!" he yelled while my body was getting smashed all the way from the bedroom floor to the living room.

"Leave me! Let go of my arm! Leave me!" I roared. I kept on screaming, asking him to release my arm.

"Get the fuck out and don't you dream of taking my son with you." He tried to kick me out of the house while wiping the floor with my weakened body. My body betrayed me and couldn't stand up to his masculine body.

He threw me on the sofa as if I were a light sack in an attempt to punch me with all his strength. I started kicking with my legs trying to push him away from me and not suffer his painful blows. One of the sandals that I was wearing slipped out of my foot and flung away under the TV stand. He continued scolding me and calling me offensive names.

While the abuse was getting worse, his mother slammed the door and entered into the house. He got off of me when he heard the door slam wide open. She started yelling at Adi saying, "I was trying to guess from which house the noise was coming until I realized it was yours. What's happened for the love of God?"

She pushed him away from me, which made him more furious. "Oh Mother, let me keep beating her! This little whore deserves to be beaten to death! I told you she's not suitable for me. She's nothing but a piece of shit!"

She walked him all the way to the bedroom and came back to check on me. I opened my arms wide open showing her the fresh bruises. "He hit me! Look at my arms, they're all red! He beat me, he beat me!" I repeated the same sentences over and over again as if I'd never learned any other words.

She stepped back to push him away when she saw him returning to the living room while shouting, "She's telling me that I am not a man! Has she ever met a real man before? Does she even have any men in her fucking family? She should've married the guy she used to know so he'd bring men home to fuck her every night."

His mother tried to calm him down by scolding him, "That's way too offensive, Adi. You have no right to say such things to her!"

Her presence didn't stop me from shouting back. "You should've married one of the bitches you knew; they'd have suited you better. Oh, wait, they all left you at the end."

I took my phone and dialed '100' to call the police. So far, I had been afraid of taking this step so I pressed on the red button to end the call. I looked for my uncle's name as I didn't want to call my father because he was still at the hospital with my sister.

The first sentence that came out of my mouth was, "Adi hit me! Please help me get the hell out of this house."

It wasn't long before Adi reacted to what he had just heard. He made his way to the kitchen and took a knife out of the kitchen drawer. "Let me see your men! No asshole will come inside this house."

His mother pulled him toward the bedroom and took the knife out of his hand.

I received a message from my sister Layal saying, "We're on our way. We'll be with you soon."

I wrote back to warn them, "He has a knife. Tell my uncle that Adi has a knife."

I didn't notice that I was repeating my own sentences from all the pressure building up inside my head and body. I couldn't even go into the bedroom to check on my son while the two of them were in there.

The front door swung open to reveal the entrance of my uncle and sister rushing to find me. "Grab your son and let's get out of here," my uncle ordered me. The time-out made Adi realize how stupidly he had acted, but that didn't prevent him from reacting awfully, as he came out to face my uncle. "Abu Ali, remember that you're in my house, and you should respect this fact."

My uncle was provoked, replying to Adi, "Who gives you the right to beat a woman? We're taking our daughter out of this house."

"I didn't beat her. She's the one who insulted me." Adi denied the abuse he had committed and continued raising his voice in an attempt to reverse what had happened by placing the blame on me.

My uncle was fighting within himself not to beat or kill him, so he turned around to face me and bellowed out a new order. "Call the police. This type of man doesn't deserve to be treated with respect."

I didn't hesitate to obey him since this is what I had tried to do before he showed up. I called the police, all the while knowing that my husband would be jailed for what he had done to me. A Hebrew speaker answered my call, but I replied in Arabic, "My husband has abused and hit me. He had a knife and threatened me with it."

The woman that answered the phone didn't speak Arabic so she forwarded my call to one of the Arab officers. The police officer asked me to repeat what I had said. He asked me to give him the address I was at, but no words could come out of my shaking body. He asked me to hand the phone to anyone around me to give him the exact address, so I handed the phone to Layal.

Layal was holding my son when she went outside to direct the two police officers who parked in the middle of the neighborhood. Two young police officers entered the house searching for me. They both had colored eyes, but the only difference between the two of them was that one of them was short and blond while the other one was tall and had dark hair.

The first thing that the blond police officer did was to lock up Adi in the bedroom to prevent any more scuffles between us. Adi's mother started screaming and yelling at us, "Where are your manners? You got the police involved! I thought we were family!" I couldn't understand how she could blame us after witnessing the big fight and after seeing my arms covered in red bruises. The brown-haired police officer made it clear that everything was being recorded on the camera mounted on his chest. He also used this camera to take photos of my arms.

Adi's mother rushed to call her husband, asking him to come over to help her solve the dilemma that Adi had put her in. He ignored her request, thinking that his wife was playing the role of a social worker trying to break up some dramatic fight. She raised her voice to make him understand how serious the situation was. "The police are here. Hurry up and come see what'll happen to your son, you old man!"

The living room filled up with more people minute after minute. The first guest to come through the door was my father-in-law. He started jumping up and down while hitting his head and screaming, "I told you to lose your bad temper! I told you that nothing good will come out of your rage!"

His daughter Salma followed to join the crazy scene that was unfolding. Her first words to me were, "You called the police on my brother? May your God be cursed!" I couldn't understand this family's obsession with cursing God's existence or referring to Almighty God as something belonging to the person they were cursing. They thought they were showing that they weren't afraid of anyone, even God Himself.

Adi's father rushed to the sofa I was sitting on and wrapped both of his arms around me, saying, "My dear daughter, don't file a complaint against your husband. I'll protect you from him. You're like a daughter to me and I am here for you. I beg you not to go to the police station. Come on, ask these officers to leave us so we can solve our problems on our own."

"He hit me. Adi hit me!" I kept on repeating the same sentence and couldn't get him away from me. I didn't have the courage to push him away even though he was suffocating me. The pressure he put on me made my hands spasmodic and my fingers froze. The brown-haired police officers realized that this old man was hurting me, but only after Layal pointed this out to him.

"Do you need us to call an ambulance?" The brown-haired policeman asked me.

Adi heard his father begging me and it drove him insane. He jumped between the walls of the room he was locked in while cursing me and asking his father to stop. Salma couldn't tolerate the situation so she attacked Layal, asking her to hand over Tahseen. This made Layal call the police officer for help. "She wants to take the baby!"

At last, the brown-haired police officer helped me break free of my father-in-law's arms by asking my uncle to take me to the police station. I went downstairs with my uncle's help with frozen hands. Layal followed us shortly with Tahseen in her arms. In the middle of the chaos, I remembered to ask for Tahseen's car seat. This forced Layal to go back to the house to get it. When she tried to enter the house, Salma slammed the door in her face to prevent her from going in. Salma's behavior provoked Layal and made her shout at her. "May God curse you! We need the car seat for the baby, you cruel bitch!"

Pestiferous Reality

I fell in love with a monster, and I ended up despising him. I thought I'd live my own fairytale, but he put me in hell instead. I gave birth to a sweet angel even though his father was a cruel devil. I was tortured throughout my pregnancy and tears were my only companion. My son heard me scream. He witnessed my abuse when he was still a young infant, but he couldn't defend me. I had to defend myself to protect the future Tahseen. Ugliness shaped the behavior of my child's father.

He called me a slut on several occasions, and he still managed to see himself as the oppressed victim in our relationship. I was dragged down the floor while my body was being smashed, and yet he thought he was the victim because I dared to say he wasn't a man. Abusing my weak body felt like a right to him.

I was harassed that night by several men, forcing me to feel that I was a piece of meat rather than a wandering soul. The abuse started at my house by Adi and continued all the way to the police station. The investigator that was supposed to help me was one of the men that had harassed me. He stopped writing down my testimony and started checking out my body, by staring at revealed parts instead of showing sympathy for what I had gone through.

"Do you usually go out like this?" He asked pointing at my sleeveless shirt.

Instead of yelling at him for disrespecting me, I confirmed that this was the way I usually dressed.

Staying at the police station for three hours disconnected me from what was happening outside with the rest of the family. I didn't have the chance to check my phone until I went back to my uncle's car. I found 30 missed calls from my father-in-law, Adi's sister, my friend Yasmina, my uncle, and two phone numbers that weren't saved in my contact list. Entering the living room of my parents' house felt as if I was entering a court session. My little cousin came running toward me to warn me that my father-in-law was there. She whispered in my ear, *He's been waiting for you for over two hours.*

I had five seconds to scan the room before finding myself surrounded by men. The first was my wicked father-in-law and two other men. I was able to recognize one of the men with Adi's father because he was Adi's friend, Raed. Raed was a certified lawyer, and his presence made sense at that moment. The other man who was sitting next to him was one of the city's important elders. Adi's father had come prepared with an army of two people hoping to end the situation that his son was thrown into. On the other hand, I had a weak team that came to the battle unprepared, and most importantly, wasn't chosen by me. There was the elder of my family, Abu Husam, in addition to two of my father's cousins. One of them was sitting on the couch wearing a white Jalabia with his hand atop a wooden cane.

Women were not allowed to speak in such gatherings unless they were asked to. Also, it was preferred not to have women in the same room as men while these were negotiating the customs that could solve the abuse I had undergone. I was allowed into that room only because I was the one who held the key that could get Adi out of prison.

Adi's father started pouring water on his face trying to get fake tears running down his eyes while asking for his son's salvation. The man in the white Jalabia who was supposed to be on my team spit out hideous words that he thought were insightful. "It won't be the end of the world if a man hits his wife. A man has the right to do so if he has to." All I was able to hear at that moment was their voices mumbling nonsense. I was placed on a couch between my father-in-law and Raed. They tried to strip me out of the people that could support me. No one assured me that everything would be okay; all of them were trying to save Adi from the hideous experience he was having in prison at that time. My younger sister Layal jumped into the living room while yelling at the so-called men who were surrounding me.

"You're forgetting the main problem. Adi hit her! He's been abusing her with his words and now he dared to take action. Are you waiting to find her dead in his hands before you can acknowledge the crime?" My father's other cousin (not the one in the Jalabia) commanded her to leave the room.

He was dressed in modern clothes on the outside, but his mentality wasn't any different from the man in the Jalabia. She refused to listen to him and turned toward Adi's father, "Your son is an abuser, and he should be punished." This time the modern cousin held her captive in his arms and forced her out of the room. We were able to hear them shouting at each other, and that made my uncle run out of the other room to stop the fight.

Abu Hussam tried to cover up what happened with Layal and asked me to break my silence to say what had happened between me and Adi. As I was about to open my mouth, Adi's father covered it with his hand begging me not to expose what his son had done. "Please don't shame us, my dear. Please don't speak." My sister couldn't stay in the other room and was able to hear what he said to me, so she broke free of my uncle and his cousin's clutches to shout again, "He's forcing her to shut her mouth. Get him away from her!"

Adi's father turned himself again toward me and lied to my face. "Please my dear, I'll do anything you want."

My feebleness made me believe him, so I said, "I want a divorce. Please help me get a divorce, Uncle."

He comforted me with more lies to make sure he would get what he wanted. "I'll force him to divorce you. You'll get everything you want from him." He pointed at the ashtray that was on the table and moved on to say: "I'll make sure he fulfills all of your rights once he divorces you. Even the ashes of the cigarette that he owes you. Please, dear! Let's go to the station and drop the complaint."

The room became more crowded when my grandmother joined the session alongside one of our close friends. Apparently, my grandmother called him in since he was a lawyer and had a good knowledge of such cases. "If you're promising her a divorce, and you guarantee that she will get her full rights, full custody of her child, and child support, then we need to write it down and sign on it before she withdraws her complaint," replied our clever friend, Qusai, to Adi's father's promises.

In return, my father-in-law had quite a talent for excluding people who weren't naïve enough for him to manipulate the situation for his own benefit. "Excuse me, may I ask who you are?" He managed to ask in a rude tone. When he learned that Qusai wasn't related to me and that he was a friend of the family, he continued mumbling, "I am sorry, sir, but this is a family issue and I think that the people who get to make such decisions are Saba's parents or her uncle."

Everyone around me started screaming to defend the presence of our friend among us while forgetting that Adi's father brought two strangers with him to a family matter. Adi's father kept on shifting between the act of shedding tears and pausing from time to time to give my sister scolding stares.

Raed leaned his head toward me and whispered in denial, refusing to believe that Adi had abused me. "Did he really hit you?"

I answered his question with an affirming, "Yes."

While everyone was fighting their way toward finding a solution for the misery Adi and his father found themselves in, my father finally entered the room with a red face that was about to explode from rage. He rushed toward me, screaming, "The son of a bitch hit you?"

As a response, I started crying confirming that he did. My father came to the rescue at last. I felt safe that he was finally with me even though I knew that he couldn't face my malicious and deceiving father-in-law. Everyone tried to calm my father down while my father-in-law kept declaring that I was like a daughter to him and that he would help me take my revenge on his own son. "Let us end the police situation and solve this matter as a family." He tried to convince us to get his son out of prison over and over again.

His request provoked my father and made him slam the table in front of him. "My daughter is free to do whatever she wants even if she wishes to keep your dog in prison!"

Everyone surrounded my father to calm him down. Meanwhile, I was lost between two options. My heart was aching due to the fact that I still loved Adi and that I didn't want the father of my son to suffer in prison. That was all because they managed to convince me that women who call the Israeli police on their husbands are considered rotten women. They used politics as a way to convince me that Palestinians should stick together and solve their problems alone, without involving the enemy and giving them a chance to torture our people. On the other hand, I knew that the men in the room wouldn't do me any justice, or punish Adi for what he had done.

The weak and kind me overcame my other inner self that wanted to face down these men.

My thoughts were interrupted when I heard Adi's father rushing me to make a decision so his son could get out of prison as soon as possible. Qusai stepped in to point out that it was late. "It's 11:00 p.m. All of the investigators who could help release him have already gone home. He won't get out tonight, even if she goes and withdraws the complaint."

The thought of Adi spending the whole night in prison was hurting me. I couldn't understand how I could worry about him when he had wronged me. I hated myself for being this fragile. I wanted to hate him, kill him, torture him, and be able to accept the idea of putting him behind bars for years. Instead, I wanted him to get out and let him be safe. The paradoxical dilemma I was having was the hardest as each of the men around me wanted to take advantage of it.

After they managed to suppress the anger and tension floating in the room, they asked me for my decision.

I broke the chaos when I announced that I wanted to get him out in return for a proper divorce that would guarantee me custody over my child and all the proper financial care for him.

"May God bless you, my dear. You made the right decision! I promise you that your wishes will be fulfilled. Can you also say that he didn't hit or touch you? Tell them that all of the tension made you think and see things that didn't actually happen."

I stared at him with shock. My sister was braver than me and yelled, "Don't lie, Saba. If you're going to do this, at least don't hurt yourself." As for me, the only response that I could manage to share was shaped by the tears running down my face.

I asked to use the bathroom before we could head out for our ugly mission, feeling as if I had to get their permission to do so. Our family friend followed me to the bathroom so he could murmur his last advice. "Don't lie, Saba. If they ask if your original statement was true, say that it was. Tell them that we made a truce based on tribal traditions. Tell them that the elders of the town had gathered and agreed to grant you a divorce and that this is why you came to withdraw the complaint. Don't listen to Adi's father; he wants to put you in jail instead of his son. This is why he's asking you to lie. You're making the wrong decision, my dear, but at least don't hurt yourself."

I washed my puffed-up face from all the tears of that day. I recalled the horrible experience I had when narrating the events of my abuse to the investigator writing down my statement. I remembered how Adi had dragged me all the way from the bedroom to the living room while hurting my arm and even wanting to hurt me more. I was hurt by the idea that my baby was on the bed in the bedroom while all of this was happening. I thanked God that he wasn't aware of the events that were happening around him. He was too pure and didn't deserve the father I had chosen for him.

Two days after the big visit to the police station, I got a phone call from the brown-haired policeman who had arrested Adi telling me that he had forgotten that he had my ID with him. "I am driving to the north to visit my family. I will call you when I get back to Jerusalem to give you back your ID."

I didn't pay attention to his intentions because my thoughts were floating in a completely other world, not noticing that he was trying to start something with me. He thought that he would get to see me again by using the excuse of my ID card. Instead, I disappointed him by sending my father to get my ID from him when he was around our neighborhood. It took him a week to find me on social media and send me a message through Facebook.

I couldn't understand how these men thought that they would be able to get something out of me by taking advantage of my vulnerable situation.

The Guy I Used to Know

Does it hurt?

Does it hurt to have someone permanently in your life like a tattoo?

Does it hurt to take this tattoo off when it's irrelevant to your life and is damaging every inch of your existence?

No one will forget your precious tattoo because it used to be part of you.

It will always leave a mark even if you remove it for good.

It's part of your story and of who you are.

I kept on replaying Adi's sentence in my head, *She should've married the guy she used to know so he would bring men home to fuck her every night.*

Adi's horrible sentence made me miss the guy I used to know. In the middle of the hate, I was feeling toward him, I remembered the love I had felt toward my ex-boyfriend.

I remembered how he used to walk me to school every day at 7:30 a.m., I remembered that whenever he would pass by any store and see something I'd like, he would buy it for me. I remembered that he knew what I liked and what I disliked, and he even knew my favorite color. We used to fall asleep together in front of our laptops every night with our cameras on. He was able to fall asleep faster than me, and that gave me a chance to watch and hear him breathe in and out. I remembered that when I used to get upset and mad at him, he would keep on calling me till I answered the phone. I wouldn't answer him until I got fifty missed calls on my phone's screen.

Having a boyfriend wasn't allowed and I had to fight for the sake of being with him at that time. I told my mother about him, hoping that she would keep my secret safe with her. Instead, she called one of my aunts to prevent me from seeing him. My mother was able to keep my secret for two days before she betrayed me and revealed my secret, "If anything bad happens to you, they'll put the blame on me. Let your family deal with you," she stated in the presence of my aunt. The first thing they did was take away my phone and laptop. They wanted to make sure that I lost everything that would help me get in touch with him.

I cried myself to sleep on that day till I woke up the next day drowning in my period blood. My feelings appeared to affect my period along with me. The feeling I had was similar to having someone put his hand inside my throat trying to take out the one I loved away from my body.

One of my friends gave me her phone at school, so I could call him. I hid in the school's bathroom to tell him that I was fine and that no one could force me to leave him.

The next time the separation attempt happened was when my aunt and grandmother saw me walking side by side with him on my way home. They didn't know that I had skipped school on that day to be with him, but they were angry to see me dressed in something other than my school's uniform. My grandmother called my name from across the street as if she witnessed an odd scene. I commanded him to leave and walk away immediately. He hesitated at first and asked me to stay and face them with me, but I refused.

I crossed the street with my heart shaking inside my body. I felt that my face and head would explode at that moment. My grandmother had her fake teeth squeaking from anger, "Go home and we'll deal with you there."

On that day, I was called a bitch for the first time in my life. I was called a whore for falling in love. My grandmother took his phone number against my will and called him. She started screaming at him asking him to leave me alone and stop seeing me. All he was able to say was, "Ok, ma'am. As you wish, Aunty." My maniac lover was able to control himself out of respect for the old lady. However, we didn't obey their commands and stayed together anyhow.

I remember my grandmother cursing the day I stepped into the zoo since he was a zookeeper. I never gave her an explanation for how I met him. All she knew was that he worked at the zoo. My handsome zookeeper used to study and work at the same time, with no luck at the end with his studies. All I know today is that he stayed where he was and never left the zoo.

The funny thing is that my son was born in the same month as my ex-boyfriend. They were both Aries.

Our relationship lasted for two years till I discovered that he cheated on me with his ex-girlfriend. He kept begging me to forgive him for the foolish mistake he made, but I couldn't despite the great love that I had in my heart for him.

I was foolish enough to tell Adi about him. As a Middle Eastern man, he wasn't able to accept the fact that another man had kissed me or touched me.

Slaughtering What Was Left of Us

For two months, I had visitors at my father's house asking me to give Adi another chance. I had blocked all of Adi's family members on social media and deleted their phone numbers. I had the courage to wipe Adi out of my phone as well. I thought that his wishes were the same as mine. I thought that he also wanted a divorce. The complete opposite happened. He pushed some of his friends to speak to me and convinced me to go back to him. He was taking baby steps, careful not to discredit or dishonor his ego.

One day after another, he started approaching my relatives. He pursued one of my father's cousins and ended up seeking the help of my father. Whenever he would come to pick up our son, he would stand with my father for half an hour asking him to convince me to come back to him or even give him the opportunity to explain himself. "I feel really guilty about what happened and I can make things right again if she just gives me another chance. Please tell her that I still love her. Tell her that separation won't be good for either one of us because we still have love in our hearts for each other. Tell her that I won't give up on her."

His words created a paradoxical dilemma inside my head. I acted as if I was disgusted by his words whenever my father would pass me his messages but deep inside his words were affecting my decisions and holding me back from going further with the separation process. I couldn't understand how I was able to still love someone who abused me physically and humiliated me. One side of me was trying to convince me that the abuse never happened and that it wasn't my beloved Adi who committed the awful acts; another part of me was trying to resist this love and think rationally. I had a battle within myself that was creating bruises all over my heart and brain.

At last, I agreed to see him and discuss what would happen next. We agreed to meet at a neutral place without our families being there to discuss things on our behalf…or that's what I thought. His words were all inspired by the agenda that his father had created for him.

He followed simple steps that helped him earn my sympathy. His plan was as follows:

- *Act as if you are as affected and oppressed as she is, and let her feel sorry for you:*
    1. *Shed a tear or two.*
    2. *Point out how much weight you've lost.*
    3. *Tell her that you keep on sniffing the clothes of your child and that you go back every night to an empty house.*
- *Remind her of the good times you had together.*
- *Explain that every couple has its ups and downs in relationships.*
- *Make her feel guilty for tossing you into prison even if it was for one night.*
- *Focus on what she did wrong so she can forget about what you did.*
- *Blame your anger issues for what happened and say that these behaviors don't resemble who you truly are.*
- *Agree to all her terms even if you're not planning to commit to any of them.*
- *Interrupt her by giving her a compliment on the way she looks even if it makes her mad.*

A sight of hope started glinting based on his words. His words built castles in the air that were too good to be true. But I believed him.

When you think that love is knocking on your door, you stupidly let it in. Even if it's a thief that will rob you of everything you have.

He clenched his hand around my wrist when we went out of the coffee shop. Both of us were standing on the sidewalk when words came out of his mouth in a strangled voice, "Saba. I ruined our life. I know that you cannot stand the sight of me right now, but deep down I know you still have love in your heart. I love you, Saba. Please take me back. I will fix everything I have broken. I will do whatever you want. Your wishes are my commands, just take me back. We had something special. Just remember the good times we had together."

"Even if I remember the special moments we had. There are hundreds of abuses and bad memories that come back to me to erase the pretty moments. If we had 10 loving moments in our marriage, then we had 100 bad incidents in return," I replied with disappointment.

"I love you, Saba," he repeated.

"Stop saying that. You're ruining what it means." I frowned.

"But I truly do love you," he insisted.

"Your actions are showing the opposite, my dear," I declared with confidence.

"Let me fix it. Let us start all over again." He kept his eyes focused on mine.

"I don't love you anymore, Adi. How can you be with someone that doesn't love you?" I looked back at him trying to convince him and myself of a bunch of lies that I wished were true.

"We've been through a lot. This is anger that is speaking, not you. I know that you still love me," he managed to explain.

"Let go of my hand, Adi. People are staring," I demanded.

"I will leave you alone now. But I beg you to think about it. We'll live somewhere isolated from everyone and start all over again. I don't expect you to interact with any of my family members if they make you uncomfortable. I'll support everything you want." He tried to buy me with lies.

I left him standing in the middle of the street watching the car I was in fade away till I disappeared from the street where he was. My voice reached the sky trying to approach god with my head smashing the back of my car seat. *Why god why? I was about to move on. Why do you put me on such tests? I am too fragile to fight this. I want to hate him, not care about him. Please don't make me break. Please give me strength to protect myself from bad decisions.*

غريبة كيف الروح اللي جواتي بتتخبط جوا جسدي، لما بتزعل بتحرقني، ولما تنبسط بتريحني. فش الها مهرب مني ولا انا الي مهرب منها.

It's weird how my soul is wallowing inside my body.
When it gets sad it burns me, and when it's happy it relieves me. It has no escape from me nor do I have an escape from it.

Al-Istikhaara Prayer

I had always heard about blind love but never believed that I'd experience it. Now I believe that you can fall blindly in love only one time in your life. It'll be the slap that will leave a mark on your heart. If you are smart enough, you will learn from what happened. If you are a hopeless romantic, you will drown in sorrow and think that life is over.

For a moment, it would feel like it's the end of the world. This moment might last six months or even a year. After healing, the broken person will re-attach the broken pieces into a new masterpiece. I started to see the light after I had left Adi, but for some reason I let part of my blinded self hold me back and make decisions for me.

Do the Istikhaara prayer. See what God will tell you. Maybe you'll find the answer you're looking for, my dear. God knows what's best for you, and he'll guide you. These were the words of my grandmother when she saw how lost I was.

Al-Istikhaara prayer is usually prayed as an attempt to seek guidance and ask God for a sign to help you decide when you are in doubt regarding taking a crucial decision that will affect your life. Muslims often do this prayer when they want to get married. One of my close friends advised me to do it before I would go ahead with my engagement to Adi. I jokingly refused, saying, *I don't want to see any sign that will drift me apart from him. I want him no matter what.* See? This is the blind love that I was describing. You even stop seeking spiritual answers because you're too attached to the person.

The signs are shown differently from one person to another. Some people have dreams, others would experience events that would give them answers, and some claim that they feel it within themselves, whether by being relieved or by having a feeling of discomfort.

I wore the headscarf and the long skirt that is designed as prayer clothes for women and prayed. After I finished the regular prayer, I repeated the Istikhaara prayer several times with my hands held high to God. I kept on repeating it even when I placed my head on my pillow to sleep.

I kept on praying for two nights in a row till I had a dream at dawn.

I was running in circles around my family's neighborhood. A maze that kept me trapped. I had a baby inside me, and I wanted a miscarriage.

I stopped to schedule an appointment via phone to go to a hospital nearby. I called a nurse who was able to get me an appointment at 2:00 p.m. I ran again trying to catch the bus to reach my destination and end the pregnancy.

I managed to get into a bus that later on transformed into a taxi. I begged the driver to go faster, but he seemed distracted and didn't have any interest in putting down the fire inside me.

The driver stopped to pick up women who were waiting in the street for a ride. I felt the taxi shrinking more and more with every second passing by while hearing the women around me giggling with the driver.

I kept on rubbing my belly trying to understand how I became pregnant. I thought to myself that if I didn't make it to my appointment, I'd be stuck with this pregnancy.

The taxi was moving, but we weren't getting close to the destination and night prevailed. The wheels kept on moving, but we were stuck in the same area. Gossip and laughter were surrounding me and no one seemed to notice my suffering as if I became invisible.

I rushed to my grandmother to seek answers. Her face turned red when she heard me narrate the events of the dream I had had. She interpreted the dream and offered me a piece of advice:

Darling, someone is trying to stall you from getting the peace and comfort you're searching for. Pregnancy in dreams means that you're carrying a weight of concerns and troubles. Miscarriage means relief and getting rid of the troubles that you have. My dear, someone is in your way and preventing you from getting the rest you need. It's a message from God, and it's up to you to decide whether to accept his guidance or continue with your plans.

You know Adi better than all of us. Deep down you know if this second chance is worth fighting for or is a waste of time. We'll support you no matter what you decide, but I hope you make the right decision, my child.

Her Shadow
Erasing or Rewriting Every Line in Our Story

I fell into the path that I was running away from. I opened a door that I was trying to lock; I opened a door of communication with Adi. His words were as sweet as honey, and he tried to win me back. Deep down I knew that this was a rainbow cloud that was hiding a storm within it. The colors blinded me and a happy smiley face was all over my halo.

We went out for lunch together as a family to go over the things that should be fixed to rebuild our house. Seeing Tahseen in his father's arms gave me the satisfaction I had been missing for the past two months. Adi assured me that everything would go as we planned and that we would be moving out of the house in a couple of months. "I need some time to rearrange the mess I created in the past months. The past two months blocked any good thoughts, and I've been suffering because my son and wife weren't with me." He blamed his laziness on us and I still felt sympathy for what we had been through. Therefore, I was able to accept his excuses for his lack of effort.

A tribe of men visited us on a Wednesday evening to assure my family that this time their son, Adi would take care of me. His father refused to join his brothers and cousins to reconcile me with my husband. I was relieved that I didn't have to see his face, but my family felt offended. After all, this man had caused damage by being present or absent from official gatherings. The gray hair that covered his head and face was a reflection of all the coffins that he had built for humans that crossed his path. In this case, gray hair on a man's face didn't resemble wisdom or noble years. He had caused injustice for the sake of building a decent reputation for himself.

My summer clothes were all packed in black trash bags, but I left everything that was related to the wintery season at my father's house. Deep down I couldn't fully commit to the act I was doing. I left half of my clothes to feel that I had the option to undo this step.

Adi was passive when the men who showed up to guarantee his bad actions wouldn't be repeated did all the talking for him. Once all the men left the house, Adi started shoving all the bags I had into his car.

I stepped into our old home expecting to have something prepared for my return. Instead, I walked into a dirty house that was dusty and rotten. Adi noticed that I was absorbing the state of filthiness that was all over the house so he fired his excuse before I even asked, "I wanted to clean it for your arrival, but I didn't have much time. I wanted to plan it all and fill the house with balloons and roses, but I am having a financial breakdown. I don't want to give you a headache tonight and bother you with all the problems I was facing while you were away."

I stayed silent, so he moved on to ruin the moment more with his solution. "I don't have work tomorrow, so we can clean it together. We'll spend the whole day together."

I nodded my head and walked into the living room while he placed the baby on one of the sofas. I continued my journey into my old home to check the state of the bedroom. I was disgusted to find that the bed had the same sheets that I placed with my own hands the last time I was at the house. "I can stand a night in a dirty house, but I cannot sleep on dirty sheets," I objected.

"I'll change them now. Don't worry about it. Where do you keep the clean ones?" He asked.

He started changing the sheets when he continued to describe the massacre that took place in the refrigerator, "I just spent my nights at the house. I couldn't spend time in it without you. A few days ago, I opened the fridge to find insects living in it so I threw out everything that was in there. I suggest that you stay away from the fridge tonight as well."

He left the room to shower. I changed my baby's diaper, gave him a bottle of milk, and placed him in his bed. I was lucky to find the crib clean since it wasn't used by anyone when we were gone. I wondered why I was so obsessed with the changes that had occurred in the house after I was thinking of leaving this life for good during the past two months. It was strange that I was upset that my old home was mistreated and no one cared about it.

Tahseen fell asleep, and I had a chance to change into something comfortable to sleep in. I chose to wear the first thing I pulled out of one of the trash bags that contained my clothes. I took a last tour around the house when I glanced at Adi praying in the living room. I was able to see that he was kneeling down and then getting up to complete his prayer. I left him to finish what he had started with God in peace. For some reason, it was hard for me to believe that someone like him would even know how to pray the Islamic way. The facts that I had ahead of me during the time I knew him didn't allow me to see the religious side of him, so I didn't know it existed.

I lay in bed hoping to fall asleep and deal with the new beginning the next day. He interrupted my plan when he moved next to me, whispering so he wouldn't disturb the baby. "I was thanking God for the second chance that I am having with you. I want to make a fresh start, and I hope that God will help us with what will face in the future. You don't know what you mean to me."

He hugged me while I stayed passive in his hands. It took me a few seconds to relax and flip to his side to hug him back. The way he kissed me that night felt as if he was afraid of losing me again. He couldn't stop his mouth from printing kisses all over my body. The night ended with us having passionate sex that cleansed our grudge and helped us freeze time to enjoy each other's company. "Why does this time feel like it's better than any time we had sex in the past?" I asked.

I heard his answer through his chest that had my heavy head placed on it. "It's because this is the first time we have sex after you're done with pregnancy. I can do some moves that won't annoy another human being who is taking a nap inside your womb. This time, it's just you and me."

"Let me know when you're not comfortable and want to sleep so I can move my head away," I mouthed.

"Are you kidding? This is the first time in months that I am comfortable and happy with pressure lying on my chest," he stated and then took a deep breath that I was able to feel.

The first two days were almost magical. Adi spent most of his time with us, helped with the house chores, and spread words on me as if he was spreading honey on bread. The honeymoon atmosphere that he created in our home lasted till he started nagging about money. As a start for his act, he had his hand on his head and uttered, "The fact that you left me made me lose focus, and I haven't done much work."

"What about your project?" I asked.

"You mean opening a studio? I need money to begin with it. I cannot afford it," he complained.

I ignored the beginning of his act to see if he would proceed with it. I named this scene: 'The Beggar and the Magic Lamp'. He used to seek my sympathy so I would help him out with all our expenses even when he wasn't in need of it.

Five minutes later, he followed me into the kitchen, sat on a seat that was next to the center table, and placed all of his attention on his phone. I started a new conversation asking him about the promises he made me. "When will we start searching for new houses?"

He raised his head to face me with his protruding eyes. "I can't understand why you hate this house. We won't find another decent house for the same price. Renting a house in Jerusalem is expensive. This house is a catch."

"But you promised me to move out of here. It's a rented house. We don't own it. Why hang on to it?" I asked with confusion.

"Is it because my family lives across from us?" He asked trying to put pressure on me.

"I just hate this house. And you promised me to be isolated from everyone around us to have a fresh start. If you think my relationship with your family will be the same after what happened between us, I am sorry to tell you that you are so wrong," I stated out loud.

This time, it was his turn to ignore me. He started to play a game on his phone. Once he finished the match he was having via phone with his friend, he added, "Were you serious when you said that you would not help me financially?"

His question forced me to leave the dishes I had in my hand and wash off the soap that was on them. "I have been paying the rent for a year. I can't recall the last time you handed me money. It had been the opposite all these years, I've been giving you money, and you didn't give me anything."

"I paid the rent while you were gone. Do you know how much money I spent with no income in my hands?" He tried to flip the table on me.

"You promised to take care of me, not the other way around," I said with disappointment.

"You knew when you got married to me that our relationship would be based on sharing and building this house hand in hand." His voice changed, trying to make me feel guilty.

"I am sticking to my word even if you won't stick to yours. I will not put any money and will no longer pay the rent. Especially for this house." I tried to remain strong.

"I cannot afford it," he simply replied.

"Aren't you the great Adi Makhlouf? Where did all your money go? Oh. I am sorry. I forgot that you had a budget for weed and alcohol," I pointed out with sarcasm.

"Watch your tone, Saba! Or are you now relying on the Israeli government to protect you?"

"Why? Are you planning to hit me again? If you touch me, I won't hesitate to call the police one more time."

"Are you threatening me?"

"You're the one that mentioned the police, not me."

He paused for two seconds, taking into consideration that our voices were too loud. I couldn't hold in and stop the fight so I moved on to ask again, "When will we move out of this house?"

"When will you wake up and realize that I lied to win you back?" He confessed with a cold and quiet tone.

I collapsed on the chair that was facing him, realizing that I had made a huge mistake.

He interrupted my thoughts when he became aware that anything he would say at that moment would affect and hurt me, "Everyone told me that a woman that throws her husband in jail is not worth keeping."

I fired back, "Everyone told me that you're nothing, but a crazy drunk that hits women."

"Well, the drunk husband of yours won't accommodate your stay at this house for free. You can either pay for your food or leave your job."

"What does my job have to do with this?"

"Don't you want me to pay for everything? Why would you need money then? And my dear, if you won't help me out, we'll move out as you wish. But don't come crying if we move into a terrible place based on what I can afford."

"Is this how your sisters are treated? Doesn't your father ask suitors to get your sisters' houses and gold? Or is it just the case with his daughters? His son's wife should contribute to everything and accept everything while his daughters should be treated as princesses."

He stormed out of the kitchen and left the house to avoid hitting me. He considered his family's lifestyle a sensitive topic. It was the forbidden garden that I wasn't allowed to bring up or enter. He expected me to respect them even when they mistreated me.

Three hours passed by and I was trapped in the horrible house that I once had escaped from. I felt the walls closing slowly in on me; I felt the windows getting wider, and I sensed the whole neighborhood whispering around me. I had no choice, but to wipe my tears and start the night routine that I usually followed to put my baby to sleep. At the end of the night, I made a truce with myself to calm down and get rid of the negative energy that was forced on me.

The lights were all off except for the light that was lashing out from the TV screen. I heard the keys make their way inside the door's lock allowing Adi to enter the house. I didn't turn my head and continued watching the movie that was streaming on one of the local channels. I was focused on Adi's moves more than the movie itself even though my eyes were directed at the TV. He checked on Tahseen and changed his clothes in the bedroom. A few minutes later, he lay down on the sofa across from me and started scrolling down his phone.

What I said about his family seemed to haunt him despite the break he had when he left the house. His solution for this grudge was pointing out one of the hidden secrets that weren't revealed to me before I had returned to him. He abandoned his phone and stared right into my eyes, "Did you know that your mother used to visit my family all the time?" He moved on to babble on how my own mother spoke badly about us. "Your own mother said that you're a terrible daughter. She also mentioned that it's common for women in your family to get their husbands jailed. It seems like a trend in the family."

I wanted to scream at him, but for some reason, my tongue got twisted and prevented me from getting words out of my mouth. His story didn't end here. He continued spreading poisonous facts. "Oh, and I forgot to tell you that someone that you know well and is really close to you used to visit my father every day for the past two months. The people that you never expect betrayal from are the ones that shock you. I've never imagined that you and your family would be this filthy."

"Why did you take me back if you think that I am a filthy person?" I asked.

"I didn't want my son to be raised with a dreadful family such as yours."

"You and your family curse God all the time and don't mind lying to get what you want and you speak about morals?"

"The shoes that my family put on every morning are cleaner than your people. You think of yourself as an oppressed human while you're the oppression itself."

"Fuck you, Adi. I hope you burn in hell."

The percussive questions and answers took a terrible path which made me escape the room and join my infant to sleep. Adi's goal was achieved. He managed to crawl under my skin. I cried myself to sleep that night thinking about the betrayal that my mother committed against me.

Every time I trusted her and thought of her as my mother, she broke my trust and thought of me as her opponent.

Mothers aren't supposed to hurt their kids. Animals are born with a natural instinct to be protective over their babies while my mother was born with a natural instinct to prey on everyone in her life.

She was born with a natural talent. She was able to read humans' weaknesses.

Once she put her hand on the person's weakness, she would squeeze on it till it bled to death.

She was a natural killer; she knew how to kill spirits, trust, relationships, happiness, and even dreams.

Her motto was *Whisper venom into their ears with a sweet and loving tone till they choked and lost their keys to comfort. Separate them so they can stay fragile and in need.*

Despite all the darkness she had in her soul, I tried to look for the bright light. Whenever I feel that I am about to reach the shining light, a breeze of air turns it down.

I played the role of a victim in all the fictional fantasies that were tailored in my head. Was it a coincidence? Or was it genetic? If it was genetic, would it be the reason behind the misery I had led myself into? I had always observed how my mother played the role of the victim in every difficult situation she faced. Tears were always a companion to her enflamed cheeks, and she would use them to escape taking the blame for anything she did wrong. She would hurt the dearest people in her heart and find her way out of the blame by acting like a fool. "I didn't mean to. You know that I don't think like you do. You know how to organize your thoughts and words. I didn't receive the same education you had."

My sisters and I used to scold her for neglecting her appearance. "Why don't you dye your hair? Why don't you wear makeup? Why don't you dress shapely or buy new clothes?" She would always blame the circumstances that were enforced on the family. "I put the house's needs before my needs. I am not like other women. I don't spend my time in hair salons or in malls. I have priorities. Plus, I don't feel that your father is generous enough to understand my need for this luxury."

I grew to understand that she did this on purpose to let us feel sorry for her all the time. She enjoyed seeing us feel bad about her gray hair that was covering half of her head. She wanted us to always pity the lifestyle she was forced to live. Whenever we would have a fight with her, she would use the subject of her having to give up luxury so we could have a fine life. This was proved when we once asked our father to give her money to do her hair. She spent the money on expensive cooking pots and kitchen tools. Being a Histrionic was my mother's choice.

I sometimes forget how much I look like her. The puffy cheeks, the colored eyes, and the soft black hair. Whenever I would have my hair up, the details of my face were revealed to be a carbon copy of my mother's face. This is why I got used to keeping it down, lying on my shoulders all the time. I didn't want to have the same neglected appearance she had.

The Crucial Dreams

My dreams were as fucked up as my real life.
I wish you a delightful flight in my fucked-up unconscious.

My aching soul was shattered into pieces. These pieces were crawling from my heart to my throat. I tried coughing them out, I tried tearing them up, but with each sonant that came out of my mouth, I felt lichen burning my throat.

I found myself sitting on a stone stool in the middle of the street next to Adi's car. I was aware that I was dreaming and living unreal events in my head. In my dream, Adi had wide, brown eyes similar to the famous Arab prose writer Al Jahiz, with gray locks occupying the edges of his head, and the fact that he was a short, masculine man was sensual. Ongoing pluvial words kept on coming out of his mouth was surrounded by his beard that had hidden grayness in it, as if he couldn't be silent for more than five minutes. I was crushed and in love with him. I glanced at him, remembering how he had opened the door for me to enter the car earlier that day and how he used 'thank you' and 'please' all the time. My unconscious at that moment felt dreadfully real.

In this imaginary story that was involuntarily woven inside my head, Adi was married and had kids. This is why he convinced me to marry him in secret without letting his wife know about our shady marriage. Men in Islam are allowed to have four wives, and this was how I became the second and hidden wife. My mother-in-law told Adi's other wife that I was the widow of his long-gone brother. She tailored an unbelievable story for us to be able to share one house.

Suspicion was all over my husband's wife; she couldn't understand the sudden appearance of me in their house. I tried to hide my jealousy and ignore the burning fire inside my heart. I did not want to be the mistress that ruined this family. She entered my room unannounced and found him sitting on my bed with a blanket covering his legs. She stared at him with fire coming out of her eyes, called him by his name, ordered him to immediately remove the blanket, and asked him to follow her outside the room. I heard their voices across the walls of my room as she screamed at him, telling him that it was inappropriate to do such a thing even if his intentions were purely innocent. His mother interfered and uttered to my husband's wife, "She is like a sister to him; do not make a big deal out of it. We're one family, and it is normal to feel comfortable in front of one another."

My husband's daughter hugged me as if I were a harmless member of this family. She was innocent and young. I figured that she was eight years old based on her appearance. After all, these events were unreal and I could assume anything I wanted. I felt ashamed whenever I used to look her straight in the eye. She had me as a role model for some reason and kept on imitating the way I dressed, laughed, and talked. I kept on thinking about withdrawing from this freaky situation.

His first wife entered my room looking in every corner as if she were searching for the hidden truth. She revealed her true intentions when she mouthed, "Your situation is weirder than weird. Why don't you return to your family's house since you don't have any children and you're not obligated to be part of this family?"

I kept on staring at her, trying to digest her sentences.

"If I were you, I would start all over again. You need to live your life not rely on others to take care of you. To be honest, I don't trust you around my husband. I see the way he looks at you and the way you look back at him."

For some reason, a tear dropped out of my eye as a reaction to what she said. She left the room after mumbling her final sentence, "In other circumstances, I would've treated you like a sister, but at this moment, I need to protect my family and keep it together. I won't let you destroy what I have."

I packed the most basic clothes in a small handbag. I dropped in my toothbrush in addition to a couple of pairs of underwear and a deodorant. I waited till the night prevailed and left the house without leaving anything behind me. I had a feeling that Adi would start searching for me. Deep down in my soul, I wished that he would suffer because I disappeared. I hated him for letting me go through this and hated myself for accepting less than I deserved.

I rested my head on a window that was placed next to my seat on a moving train. I was moving to another city aiming toward nothingness. A prostitution house was where I found myself with a wig on my head. I was no longer myself. I tried my best not to sleep with men. I manipulated them and convinced them that I had slept with them even though I hadn't. I had two methods, I would either let them get drunk until they wouldn't remember what happened or drug them by adding a couple of drops of liquid to their drinks.

Nothing made sense in this dream, but it didn't seem to be over.

Strange men visited the house where I was staying, and others were sharing the place with us. I was on the right path of collecting money without getting touched. I was deceiving men and prostitutes to think that I was part of their world. Unfortunately, I couldn't deceive the guard who was sitting outside my room. He was able to figure out my tricks.

The guard and I exchanged gazes. At first, I interpreted these stares as a threat. I thought that he would either expose my lies or take advantage of the situation. The opposite happened, he started helping me. Prostitutes used to knock on my door on a daily basis. I had never opened the door or replied to their screaming. I would climb on a chair to reach the gap that was between the ceiling and the door to see who would be knocking on it. I heard the guard yelling at them, telling them to leave my room alone.

I couldn't figure out the point of saving all that money. I convinced my dreaming self that I was hiding to make my husband miss me, I wanted him to go crazy, and I wanted him to realize that he would not be able to live without me. After all, I was his wife and he should bring me out to the light so people could see who I was to him.

When I woke up from these missy events that were shaped by my subconscious, I had a weird feeling that Adi's first wife who was trying to kick me out of the house was actually Adi's real mother. I didn't remember the face that resembled Adi's first wife in the dream, but it just felt that it was Adi's mother. She resembled the shape of the jealous woman who wanted to possess Adi and keep him for herself.

Next Deadly Dream

My hands were covered.
My hands were red.

Face covered with salty tears.
Eyeliner melting on my cheek.

Blood was leaking on my wrist.

I was shaking.
My soul was aching.

Adi was dead.

I woke up covered with sweat and started breathing heavily. It took me seconds to realize that I had had a nightmare. I started crying about the fictional murder of my husband, I didn't want to commit a crime in order to escape this hell.

Gluing Broken Pieces or Ending a Disaster

The on-and-off fighting lasted for a month and a half. I relived the scene of my honeymoon when I had to lock myself in the bathroom to cry and scream on the inside so no one would hear me. He didn't have any intensions to fix what was broken, and I was in defense mode. Whenever he would attack me with vicious words, trying to wound me, I would turn into a street fighter and fire back at him. We made each other miserable. He needed an obedient woman who would suck it up and treat him like a king after he would pour all his garbage into her soul. As for myself, I needed a shoulder to lean on; someone who would stick to his words and do as promised.

Adi's family tried to punish me for throwing their son in jail. They looked at their precious son as the one who settled for less than he deserved. His father avoided me most of the time and made sure to hide in his room whenever I would pass by their house. I tried to limit the times that I had to stop by their house and made my visits last for less than half an hour. On the other side, Adi's mother would break into our house at odd times, trying to pass me a message that this was her son's house, not mine. She would come over at night, claiming that she missed Tahseen. She would awake him from his sleep just to tease me. She knew that I had a difficult time putting him down to sleep, and she loved breaking the rules just to make me burn on the inside. Adi would remind her that it was his bedtime and that we shouldn't wake him up, but she would ignore the hints. The people who promised my dad that they would treat me like their daughters took their son's side even though he mistreated me.

"If you think that your family and I will reconcile again, you're wrong my dear," I repeated to Adi several times.

The sun broke through the windows of the house on a Sunday morning. We had one of our usual fights the previous night; therefore, electrical tension surrounded us the next morning. "I'm going to take Tahseen to say good morning to my mother," he stated from the living room. I stayed in bed till he stormed out of the house. I was able to get to the kitchen and make coffee to start my miserable day at the revolting house.

It wasn't long till he returned to the house and got dressed to leave for work. For the first time since we were married, I cherished that we didn't have mutual weekends or off days. He stood across from where I was sitting and asked, "What will you do today?"

I didn't give him any attention and started searching for something to watch on Netflix.

He moved on to state, "I placed Tahseen in his bed."

I didn't reply to this statement, and it drove him crazy. Ignoring him made him shout, "Fuck you and fuck your mornings" and slammed the door behind him.

I wanted to hit myself in the face. I wanted to take away my life. Crazy ideas were swimming their way into my head and thoughts. "It's either you settle down at this shithole and accept your destiny, or you get out now and never return. You need to make a final decision and stick to it," I yelled at myself.

I waited till my son had fallen asleep, packed essential clothes and belongings, and called a taxi. I asked the taxi driver to park away from our building to avoid being seen by Adi's mother. I went up and down the stairs seven times till I was able to get everything I packed out of the house. Red lines shaped as bruises all over my arm because of all the disposable bags that I carried all the way from the house. I couldn't let the taxi driver get near the driveway of the house, so I had to get all the bags all the way to where he had parked.

I managed to get all of my clothes and basic stuff out of the house. I had to sneak out this time to be able to get what belonged to me. The previous time, I had Adi's sister Salma in the bedroom with me monitoring everything I had taken. They treated me as a thief at my own house, thinking that I would take what wasn't mine. The irony was that most of the things at the house were bought by me and my family. They were guarding what was originally mine.

I called my siblings to meet me on the street to help me carry Tahseen and get everything I had into their house. I was lucky enough to find young boys playing football in the street. They all came running toward the taxi offering to help carry the bags to the house.

Haya took Tahseen out of my hands and sat next to me trying to understand what was happening. "I called Dad. He's on his way," she assured me. She glanced at my arms and saw the bruises I had. "I will kill the son of a bitch. Did he hit you again?"

"It's from carrying all these bags by myself. Each time I went down the stairs I had 4 bags hanging on my arms and hands," I responded.

"Don't cover for him. You can trust me with this," she continued.

"I swear to god that he didn't hit me this time. He's too afraid to go to jail again." I tried to make it believable even though the bruises seemed as if someone had tried to tie me up somewhere. The universe was playing against Adi with the signs that were in my arms, even though he had nothing to do with it this time.

My phone rang, and it was a text message from Adi:

Send me a list of the groceries that we need for the house. *12:13*

I found it strange how he shifted moods between each text, each call, and during different moments.

I ended up saying my goodbyes via text instead of in person. Even though I had the courage to leave the house, I guess deep down I was still afraid to face him.

Don't even bother. I left the house. *12:30*
We can end this peacefully
or we'll have to open a case through court *12:30*
We can agree on days and times for you to see the baby 12:31
and on how to divide his time between us. *12:31*
Life between us is unbearable and I cannot resist anymore. *12:32*
I wish you nothing but the best in your life. *12:32*
It's better if we end this in a civilized way and avoid the chaos of courts. *12:33*

He called me to scold me, "You'll return home the same way you left."

"Adi, I am not coming back. This is the last time," I replied with a suffocating tone.

"I am not in the mood for your childish games. I expect you to be home once I get back," he demanded as if his wishes should be commands.

"I am serious. This is it. I no longer can play this game. I cannot bear getting to this level with you again. This is not the life I wish for myself or for our child," I added.

He didn't want to believe that this was happening. The denial lasted till he returned home and found our closet half empty. At that time, he sent me a new text message: "At least don't block me so we can agree on the times that I'll get to see the boy." 16:00

The Harvey Specter of Jerusalem, October 2018

My sisters were alert to the fact that I was walking, speaking, and acting like a zombie. I needed an escort to help me through my hunt for a lawyer. Layal started calling every person we knew to help us find a foxy lawyer who wouldn't be manipulated by my father-in-law. "We need someone Adi's father cannot buy. He's a person of power and has connections across Jerusalem," Layal would emphasize in every call she would make.

We were guided to see a famous lawyer in East Jerusalem, known for his malicious personality. His specialization was Family Law which included divorce cases, and his area of power was the Sharia Law.

We were able to get an appointment to meet the arrogant bastard who thought he was the cleverest man in Jerusalem. We entered his rotten office neglected and with old furniture.

He made us wait for ten minutes, so he could make an entrance and impress us. His secretary/son-in-law informed him that we were waiting for him in his office. He entered the hideous office that was missing the sun's light to find two young girls waiting for him. First, he glanced at my sister Layal who had her hair in a boyish ponytail, and then shifted his eyes toward me. Layal remained silent while I narrated my case to him.

He asked me to hand him my Islamic marriage certificate to see what was agreed on when we had it done. Layal interrupted his reading session to ask, "Do you know who her father-in-law is?"

He denied that he knew him. Layal moved on to declare his full name, but he didn't give her questions any attention as if he was ignoring this fact on purpose.

After he scanned the marriage certificate, he started wording while writing down what he could get me if I hired him. When he got to the point of mentioning the gold, he asked me, *"Did you get all the gold that is mentioned in the contract?"*

"He gave me 70 grams out of 200 grams," I answered.

"Then you should get the rest of the gold that he didn't give you," he replied.

The list he had on the A4 paper was as follows:

- ❖ 130 grams of gold.
- ❖ 5000 Jordanian Dinars as your dowry.
- ❖ 5000 Jordanian Dinars for the furniture. He can either give you the furniture that he bought you for the house or he can pay the 5000 Dinars.
- ❖ Alimony for you as a separated woman who still didn't get a divorce. He has to pay 1400 NIS each month for you, starting from the day you left the house.
- ❖ Alimony for the child that can get up to 1400 NIS.
- ❖ Your alimony for three months after you get divorced which is 1400 NIS for each month.
- ❖ Full custody of the baby.

After he declared what he could get me, he handed me the paper that had all the information he hand written.

Layal repeated the same question again, "You never heard about her father-in-law? He's a well-known man in Jerusalem."

He stopped speaking for a minute while his facial expression shifted to a thinking mode. "Wait a minute. His head is covered with gray hair. I mean his hair is all white." He suddenly remembered.

"Yup. He's the one with all the gray hair," Layal confirmed.

"Wait a minute," he excused us to leave the room and call for his son-in-law. "Hassan. Hand me the pink note that we wrote a few days ago." We heard him scream this request to his secretary Hassan.

Once he returned to the room, he read out loud from the pink paper that was apparently ripped out of a notepad: "Saba Mousa Mohammad Salim."

"Yes, this is my full name. Who gave it to you?" I asked with confusion.

"Your father-in-law visited me a few days ago and asked me to refuse to have you as a client if you consider hiring me," he said with a smirk on his face.

I couldn't think clearly or know how to react after he released this information. Layal noticed how nervous and uncomfortable I was, so she had the lead in the conversation instead of me. "But we want you on our side. We don't want anyone else." She tried to feed his ego.

"Don't worry about it. My son is a lawyer as well. We can both take your case," he asserted.

"You mean you'd both have us and the Makhlouf family as your clients?" Layal asked trying to see if she had misunderstood him.

He answered Layal by nodding his head, while his hands were knotted together. Layal decided that this was the end of the conversation. She stood up and I followed her lead again. She leaned toward his desk and grabbed the paper he had written everything. She held the paper against his face and uttered, "In case you consider pleading against us, please remember that you'll have to plead against your own words that are documented on this piece of paper."

His foxy face expressions changed after Layal's statement. He was in complete shock. Apparently, he thought that since we were young girls in an oppressive society that was followed by men, we would take his words for granted and not understand when someone would try to deceive us.

"Does he think we're stupid? Is it even legal to have both of us as his clients for the same case?" Layal yelled out in anger when we left the horrible building.

I sat on a stone that was placed on the side of the street that was facing the building. I couldn't help, but cry over the fact that each man I met for my case was trying to manipulate me.

My sister crouched down toward me to scold me for breaking down. "It's still your first station. You have a long way ahead of you that is filled with rocks and traps. You should expect the worst from people around you until this war is over. You're your own savior. If you don't wake up, you will fall hard, my dear. Where is the woman who left her house with all her belongings by herself? You need to bring back this woman."

I tried to absorb every word she said, but couldn't hold in the tears. She leaned closer and hugged me while we had a pedestrian crowd observing our scene. I couldn't see them; they became invisible to me. They no longer mattered in the bubble of sorrow that I was captured in.

The dramatic scene ended when I giggled with tears filling my eyes, "What kind of person doesn't like watching friends? This should be enough of a reason to get divorced." I tried to swallow the pain and stand up on my feet.

I was about to lose hope, based on all the weird names and recommendations that I received from people around me. Each person gave me a different name, and most of the people I called would end the call by saying, "But we don't guarantee that your father-in-law won't buy this lawyer."

The meaning of 'buy him' here stands for the power of persuasion that my father-in-law had on people. He was able to buy people with his words and recruit them to his side.

In the end, I trusted our family's friend Qusai. I couldn't forget how he stood by my side the night Adi was jailed. I was reassured when he yelled in my ear through the phone, "He's the Harvey Specter of Jerusalem."

"Who's that?"

"He's a famous character in a TV show called 'Suits'. Harvey Specter is the ultimate lawyer who never loses cases or gives up on his clients. Harvey fears that his name would be smudged if he betrays his clients. He can't risk losing his glamorous reputation. This lawyer is the same as Harvey. But I must warn you, he's a little bit expensive."

"Did you lock the door?" I'd ask Adi every night before we would go to sleep.

You know what the hardest part was? To be lost in the chaos, forcing yourself to be strong while you're being attacked by the sweet memories you shared together. Even the smallest details visit you in weird and uncomfortable times. I was sitting on a chair in the lawyer's fancy lobby when I remembered how Adi and I used to ask each other if the house was locked or not at night. He would leave the bed to double-check, even if he'd be sure that it was locked just to assure me that we were safe.

I walked into the lawyer's office terrified, knowing that it was still the beginning of the war with Adi. The Harvey Specter of Jerusalem offered me something to drink as an opening to our conversation. "Water would be great. Thank you," I replied. He buzzed in his secretary to bring me a glass of water.

"I understood from our previous phone call that you want to get divorced?" He inquired.

I managed to act strong, even though my voice was shaking. "Yes. I no longer want to stay married to my husband."

He paused for a minute examining me and asked, "How old are you? You look too young for a woman seeking a divorce."

"I am 27. No one likes to end their marriage, but sometimes things get out of hand, and we are forced to make such decisions."

"How long have you been married?" He asked.

"For a year and a half so far."

More questions followed trying to understand my case. "Did he physically abuse you?"

Tears joined my answer this time when I uttered the word, "Yes. And he was jailed for one night only because I withdrew my complaint." I hated having to tell everyone around me that I was abused. Saying it out loud made me feel weak and ashamed.

I tried to summarize my story to this stranger in five minutes, trying to cover all the important elements of it. I emphasized the fact that Adi wanted at some point to take my son away from me. "What matters the most to me is to have the custody of my son. I don't want Adi to take him away from me. He is six months old."

"Your son is under the age of two. Of course, you'll have full custody. If you hire me, I guarantee that he will stay with you even if one day you decide to get married again. You're still young and life is ahead of you. However, you need to understand that without a court order, you'll be under the threat of losing him. This is why everything should be documented through the court. The words of your ex-husband are considered bullshit if they're not documented. Also, the fact that he had been jailed can be an asset to your case." He moved on and explained the process he would follow. "We will file for the custody of the baby; we will file for your alimony and for child support for the baby. He'll have to pay you alimony until the day he divorces you. We will pressure him with all the expenses that he'll have to pay if he doesn't divorce you."

He stopped speaking and started writing down the amount of money he would charge me for each case he would plead. My brain couldn't convert the amount of 7500$ to Shekels because of all the information I was trying to memorize.

I mentioned the name of Adi a couple of times, and the name rang a bell in his ears.

"You're married to Adi Makhlouf?"

I nodded my head as a sign of affirmation.

"How did you dare to enter the golden cage with Adi Makhlouf?"

"Love made me dare."

"But his reputation is fishy and smells like rotten cheese. Sorry for the nasty description, but this is how bad his reputation is."

He took a deep breath and reproached, "Adi Makhlouf."

"Do you still love him?" He asked.

"No. I don't," I replied.

"Do you love him?" He repeated the question.

"No. I no longer do," I assured him.

"I am asking because I don't want you to go through the whole process if there is still a slight chance that you'll go back to him. It's not an easy road. You need to be strong and know what you want from the beginning. If you say that you don't, it means that I can start working on your case," he explained.

I confirmed again that I was 100% sure that I wanted to go through the divorce process.

"I don't want you to waste your money if you're uncertain. This is why I asked if you still love him," he forewarned.

He ended the session with one last information: "If you hire me, I would plead your case through the Israeli Family Court. I don't do Sharia Law."

The first thing I did once I left the lawyer's office was call my sister Layal. She started asking the questions that I had already asked myself.

"Do you have the money he's asking for? How will you pay him?"

"I can sell the jewelry I have as a down payment and the rest can be paid as monthly payments."

"I'd rather that you don't sell your gold. Keep it hidden till you actually need it or even keep it for yourself."

"I don't want anything that would remind me of him. I want to sell it."

"What about your savings? Why don't you use them?"

"I need a car to move around. I feel as if I am tied down and can't move freely with Tahseen."

A curious question followed all the technical questions that Layal had: "How does he look? I am curious to know what he's like."

"He's very tall and is the opposite of the first lawyer that we met. He's also thin and his suit was on point. His suit appeared very expensive, unlike the cheap suits that we saw on other lawyers. I wasn't focused on his appearance, but I remember that his eyes were colored. He looks fine for someone his age. I guess he's in his late forties." I satisfied her curiosity with the details that I was able to remember from one session.

Love Vs. Hate

You know what love is?
It's being surrounded by hundreds of people and still feeling miserable because one person is absent.
You know what love means?
It means that you cannot have happiness even though everything around you is amusing, but you'll desire the misery you feel when you're around your beloved person.
You know what hate is?
It's when you hate a person because you love him/her.
Do you know what hate means?
It means that you hate him/her for reminding you of all of your memories together while you're apart from each other.
I hate you for walking into my life.
I hate that you're the reason behind my misery.
I hate that I see everything as darkness because of you.
I hate that you're the reason for depriving me of the optimism I had for life.
I hate being alive because of you.
I hate that I disbelieve the abuse you committed against me.
I hate that you have cut me in half. A half that is still hanging on and wants to live and another half that wants to die and end my life.
You're the asshole that made me fall in hate and made me despise the greatness of falling in love.

The Fool and the Charming Husband
~Part 1~

It's an obstacle that you need to go through. I know that it'll be annoying to sit around him again while someone else is trying to fix your marriage for you. If you really don't love him, you'll overcome this block and jump off it easily. If you still have love in your heart for him, he might drag you down and hold you back. That was the explanation that the lawyer provided regarding the first step that I needed to take at the Family Court. "The Family Court believes in second chances. They give couples an opportunity to have sessions with a social worker who can give them solutions for the obstacles and hardships they face in their marriage. It's something forced upon us, and we cannot skip it. Just keep on confirming that you no longer want to fix this marriage and explain the reasons why," he added.

A warning followed: *Don't agree to sign anything before you hand it to me for review. She might offer you a deal that you both would want to agree on. She will try to give you a weekly schedule that would have the official times that he gets to see his child. Even if you find it convenient, tell them that you want to consult with your lawyer first. Don't sign on anything, even if you think that it's harmless.*

My journey got me introduced to several waiting rooms. The one I was waiting at for our first session with the social worker smelled like a dentist's clinic. It was big enough and had a rounded desk in the middle of the room for what appeared to be designated for the secretaries of the office. My heart pulses were beating fast as if I were expecting a meeting with the angel of death. I hated how weak my body became around him and how it betrayed me on several occasions. Especially, when my eyes shed tears against my will and when my voice would start shaking like a belly dancer, making my words seem irrational.

Adi made an entrance and sat as far as he could away from me. We didn't look at each other. He was wearing the same outfit that he had worn on our first date. The black T-shirt looked pale from being washed several times throughout the years. I couldn't understand why he was attached to it.

The social worker came out of one of the rooms that later on turned out to be her office. She went straight toward the secretaries' desks to confirm our names and one of the secretaries pointed at us.

She called our names and asked us to follow her to the office. Adi and I left an empty chair between us, refusing to get close to each other. The social worker started the session by asking us to introduce ourselves. Adi started bragging as usual about his work as if he were the god of photography. He was self-focused and elaborated on the themes of the exhibitions that he had held in past years. The social worker was astonished by Adi's work and seemed to be familiar with his name. After all, my beloved husband knew how to do good marketing and advertisements for his work. On the other hand, my introduction was brief.

"As I see in your file, I understand that you're the one who filed for the alimony case," the social worker stared at me pointing out this fact.

I nodded my head as a 'Yes'.

"Are you separated or do you live under the same roof?" She asked.

"She's now staying at her parents' house," Adi answered on my behalf.

She continued asking a set of questions to understand our living situation including our baby's.

"How often do you see your child? And are you facing problems regarding this matter?" She steered the question toward Adi.

"Whenever I ask for the baby, she lets me take him. She's flexible in this matter, and I thank her for this," Adi answered.

The questions were rotated toward Adi and me, and Adi took care of answering most of the questions. I tried to distract her from myself and push away the tears that were about to run down my cheeks. I glanced at her, trying to memorize her features instead of focusing on the thought of crying. She had short wavy hair, and brown eyes, and her eyeliner didn't seem to match. I focused on her eyeliner and how it was smudged on her eyes. She was curvy, and the loose pink shirt seemed to cover the details of her body as if it was intended for it to be this way. I started questioning the scarf that was tied to her neck and couldn't tell if it was a fashion trend or if it was there to distinguish it as her own unique style.

Adi's phone interrupted my thoughts when it started ringing. The social worker felt offended and stated that we should turn off our cell phones throughout the sessions because the information that was being shared was considered confidential.

"Why do you want to end this marriage?" She slowly rotated her chair toward me when she asked this question.

"I no longer feel safe to be under the same roof with him. I've been physically and verbally abused," tears joined my answer, despite all of my attempts not to cry.

Adi was used to seeing me cry all the time. He described it as one of my famous qualities. He had always been able to describe my misery as being *MY THING*: "It's her thing to cry. She once told me that she's a crying baby and that she cannot control her tears. She even told me to disregard her tears, since part of her personality is to cry over everything." He proudly used my words against me in the presence of the social worker. It was easier for him to believe that this was part of my personality rather than to see the truth. He couldn't confess to himself that since the day he married me, my tears had never dried. "I didn't abuse her; it's all in her head," he added.

The social worker asked Adi to leave the room, so she could have a one-on-one discussion with me, and explained that he would be next. She needed to hear our story separately and then hear it by having us both in the same room together.

"If you want to end this marriage and you're convinced that you no longer want him, then why are you crying?" She asked to provoke me as if she was expecting a hidden fact behind my tears.

"I don't know," I simply answered.

"If you truly don't want him, then why are your tears present in the conversation?" She asked again.

"I cannot control my tears when I feel pain or discomfort. His presence brings back all the bad memories that we had together," I clarified.

"Can't you remember the sweet memories?" She asked when she leaned to hand me a tissue.

"The bad ones are covering all the good ones that we had together," blowing my nose followed this answer this time.

She paused for a second, took a deep breath, and boldly asked, "Is there someone else in your life?"

I didn't feel safe, and I felt that she had me under a microscope, trying to flip the table on me. All of her questions made me feel as if I abused him not the other way around by wanting to end a toxic relationship.

"No, I don't have or want anyone else in my life. Knowing him made me lose faith in men in particular and in marriage in general. I just want to feel safe and rest in peace," I explained.

"Marriage is hard and you cannot give up because of the first obstacle you face. You can fix what was broken. However, fixing this marriage needs both parties to be involved and you must have the desire to want to make it work." She started lecturing me on the essence of marriage making me look like a spoiled girl that wanted to run away from obstacles instead of focusing on the abuse. She disregarded that I needed to be saved not criticized.

I went to the bathroom when Adi entered the room for his turn. I stared through the mirror at the smudged eyeliner that seemed to be part of my style whenever I grapple with a problem. I had makeup on to cover my puffy eyes to show that I was strong and that his absence didn't affect me, but my tears reflected another story.

I rejoined the session with dry, natural, and clean eyes.

"Saba, your husband wants you back," the social worker stated. "She moved on to offer us her help with marriage therapy. Take advantage of my help. I am here for you. I have had couples come with bigger problems and I helped them get out of their misery. However, these sessions won't make any difference in your lives if one of you doesn't put all of your efforts into it. It takes sacrifice, and each person needs to acknowledge the bad habits they have."

I interrupted her to decline the offer in a polite manner, but Adi refused to accept that I rejected the generous offer. "Saba, I am not going to tell you to do it. For the sake of our child, I am asking you to accept it because I believe in us."

"Please stop. I cannot do this. It's over." I tried to end the begging before it started.

I knew that he wanted to win her sympathy and show me as the bad person in the relationship. His plan was working; I was able to see the judgmental looks that the social worker had because she was only able to see the surface of our marriage. She saw a loving husband who made a mistake, and who was willing to fix it. On the other hand, she viewed me as a cruel wife who had fallen out of love because of another man.

"The clock is ticking. We need to wrap up the session," she said firmly.

"You have two options. You can either end everything here or avoid going through the endless court sessions, or you can choose to go through the marriage therapy and ask the court to put your case on hold till we see what will happen with the therapy. If you choose the therapy, and in the middle of the sessions you see that it's not working for you, you can end it and get back to the court to follow up on the case," she added.

"Can we agree on everything with you? Even the custody of the child and the alimony?" I asked.

"Yes. If you both agree on a certain agreement, we can end everything together, send your agreement to the court, end the case, and grant you a divorce. As a matter of fact, I want to discuss with you the times that Adi will be permitted to see his child," she clarified.

We were able to agree on the times according to both of our schedules. It wasn't a hard case, given the fact that I didn't want to prevent Adi from seeing his child. However, it didn't go smoothly when we got to the money part. The amount of money I asked for bothered Adi and the social worker seemed to agree with him. "Can you please explain why you're asking for this amount of money? You cannot memorize a number given by your lawyer without understanding what is it for." She started scolding me for asking for something without clarifying the reasons behind it.

"I am asking for a temporary alimony for myself as a wife till he divorces me, for my child, and for the expenses of the place where we are currently living," I tried to explain myself.

"You're currently living at your parents' house. You're not paying rent. I don't think you get to ask for money if you're not renting a place of your own," she challenged me with a fact that I knew otherwise.

I remembered clearly that Adi should be responsible for the living accommodations of his child, even if he was living at my family's house. I recalled my lawyer's advice when they were objecting to the money matter, "We want money to be a blockade that he would want to escape. This way, we will guarantee that he will not keep you on hold and divorce you. Don't let them provoke you with their words. If he keeps you on hold, he'll have to pay alimony for you as a wife. If he chooses the easy way, he'll divorce you and keep paying for his child only."

I snapped out of my thoughts to hear him discussing his bad income. "My work depends on the different seasons. I don't have a stable income like everyone else. If it's wedding season, my income would be great, but if it's winter, then I don't have much income. I try to save some of the money I make in the high season for the leaner times."

The social worker handed us the custody agreement that had the times that Adi would get to spend time with his child and asked us to sign it. I refused to sign until my lawyer would review it. She accepted my request and looked back at Adi to pass him a piece of advice, "I recommend that you hire a lawyer as well."

Adi dared to break the silence that was roaming between us and started speaking to me as we were waiting for the elevator, "Saba, we can fix this. This lady is our gift from heaven to help us rebuild our marriage. I still love you and I still want you."

"Adi, please let us end this in a civilized way. I no longer wish to be with you. We're over," I replied.

Adi started raising his voice when he noticed that the social worker was making her way to the bathroom that was next to us. "I love you, Saba. Please give me a second chance. I promise to do whatever you want this time."

"Please. Stop," I whispered.

The elevator door opened and we had to walk into it at the same time. Adi's body was getting closer to mine when he was trying to convince me to go through the therapy sessions as a last shot, "We shouldn't ignore such an opportunity."

"Please keep a distance between us," I requested.

As a result, he apologized and took a step back.

His attempts to get a glance of hope continued till we made it to the main street.

"Adi, do you think that I am thrilled that we're getting a divorce? No one likes to break his family, but ours is already broken. This is why it's better to end things here before it gets worse and we make ourselves and our son miserable. We still can be friends for the benefit of our child. We should maintain healthy communication for the sake of Tahseen." I gasped the words out loud.

A new form of begging began for another ten seconds till he realized that he was being rejected for the hundredth time. This made him switch his tone and his facial expressions from a weak person to a monster who wanted to gain back his dignity that had been lost in the last ten minutes. His face was close to mine when he shifted to attack mode and mouthed, "Who do you think you are? You're nothing but a spoiled brat that wasn't raised well. You're a rude girl that needs to learn how to talk and behave."

I couldn't understand what happened and how he was able to change his personality that quickly. I asked him to get away from me and walked away as fast as I could. I leered back and saw that he was passing his hands through his hair and touching his face from irritation. To calm himself down, he lit a cigarette to breathe out all the angry energy that was rolling all the way from his head toward the rest of his body.

I called my lawyer to update him on what had happened with the social worker and mentioned what had happened with Adi. The first thing that the lawyer did was analyze Adi's intentions, "Such behavior is expected from such a person. He wants you back to mistreat you again and get his revenge. Don't think that all this begging is because he loves you. It's because he wants to win this battle and break your head once you get back to living under the same roof with him."

The Fool and the Charming Husband
~Part 2~

"I don't want to continue with this." I inhaled and exhaled the sentence with tears.

"What's wrong? We didn't even begin the session," Salwa asked.

"I don't have a degree in psychology, and I don't want to study the different personalities that he has to continue with this marriage. This is bigger than me."

"What happened?" She pointed the question toward Adi but he chose to remain silent.

"When we headed out after our last session with you, he started begging me and telling me how much he loves me. The begging and loving kept on going till we got to the street, and he shifted personalities. He changed into someone else in seconds and started calling me bad names," I replied.

"You don't understand how irritating she is. I am trying my best to make this work and she's careless." Adi tried to put the blame on me.

"I know what that was about, Adi. You couldn't accept her rejection so you fought back by describing her as a bad person. This is your defense mood," Salwa gave a brief explanation.

"I won't try to defend myself, but I should point out that a well-behaved lady doesn't curse. If only you could hear the swear words she uses when she's angry. Is it possible to say them so you can see how bad her language is?" Adi tried to attack me thinking of my swear words as an excuse for his behavior.

"Stop recalling our past fights. Did I use any swear words last time against you?" I asked, with irritation and anger.

"Let me tell Madam Salwa what language you used whenever we had fights," he continued with the clashing excuses.

"I don't want to hear the swear words. Our goal is to focus on the present, not the past," Salwa tried to end the current discussion.

"If you think that she's a bad person, why do you want her back?" Salwa interrupted Adi after he had rambled for fifteen minutes about how terrible I was as a person and as a mother.

He disregarded her question and continued condemning me as a bad mother and on how I was prioritizing my work over my child.

"You keep on criticizing her motherhood instead of focusing on the good things that she's doing for your child." She tried to hold a mirror with her words so he could see the accusations he was making against me.

"Mothers should focus on their children and put their needs ahead of theirs. In her case, she's choosing herself and her career over our child." He couldn't stop stabbing my motherhood in the gut, and he went on to lecture us on what good mothers usually do.

"Adi, working mothers deserve the same applause that housewives get. You won't be fair if you compare the parenting methods or affections that may be given by different people." She defended my case since she had the same situation as I did. After all, she was a working mother who knew how challenging it was to keep a balance between her private life and work.

I stayed silent knowing that he wouldn't appreciate anything I had been doing to my child. Therefore, I shifted my thoughts to a different place as I had in the last session. The social worker didn't give me a chance to analyze a new outfit since she was wearing the same pink shirt with the same scarf wrapped around her neck.

"What about you, Saba? Will you consider marriage therapy?" She called me out of my subconscious.

"I believe that I am protecting my child from the life he would have if Adi and I stayed together under the same roof. It's better for him to be treated well by both of us while we're separated than be traumatized by our fights and by the anger issues that Adi has," I responded.

Adi jumped in to defend himself, "You're not that great yourself when it comes to anger issues. You sure know how to fire back."

The second session ended on a narrow thread that my word was holding it together. It was up to me to decide whether to give my marriage another chance or stick to my decision.

Adi made sure to humiliate himself in the middle of the street hoping that I would feel bad for him. His target was achieved successfully. My heart was torn into pieces trying not to be affected by his pity talk.

"You don't know how much you mean to me. I know that I am not that great at expressing myself or showing the love I have in my heart for you. This is just who I am. I'll work on this I promise. I'll also work on my bad temper." He tried to make a statement as one single tear fell from one of his eyes. He made sure that I was able to see this singular tear.

"I'll think about it. Please don't pressure me into doing something that I don't feel comfortable about," I replied.

"Ok. Think about it. This is all I am asking for." His sentence was bursting with hope, and it made me feel that I was the bad person in the story.

My brain was trying to prevent me from going forward with a step that would break me, and my heart was fighting the truth.

The Fool and the Charming Husband
~Part 3~

I had no control over my thoughts. The clock that was hanging on the wall at the end of the class had most of my attention. I ran out of class as soon as the bell rang to make the crucial phone call. "Madam Salwa, I want to go through marriage counseling," I uttered a simple sentence that would lead to disappointment or to a success story.

It wasn't long till I received a text message from Adi telling me that he was really thrilled when the social worker called him to confirm that our next session would include marriage therapy. I couldn't share the same shining enthusiasm he had. My feelings were cold and colored blue.

"Please don't expect much from my side," I wrote in a reply to his message.

"Your father traumatized you and treated you badly your whole life and my mother's shadow is still following me everywhere I go causing me harm. I accepted you as you are and wanted to create something special together away from their damaging acts. But you're used to tyranny and want to relive the past of your father. I am not a repeated mistake. I am alive to fix the history," I emphasized my first statement during our first marriage counseling session.

"My father is the elder of the family and men with mustaches follow his lead. Why should I go against his words and his life experience?" He proudly responded.

"I agree with Adi on this point. He shouldn't disobey his father. It's a social, tribal, and religious point that you should respect." The social worker affirmed as if I dared to scratch the gospel truth.

"I am not asking him to disobey his father. I am asking him to separate between the two families and not mix things together. He can have a great relationship with his parents and at the same time not let it affect his own family," I tried to explain my point knowing that it wouldn't make a difference.

"We're in a Middle Eastern society where some things cannot be argued against. You should try to understand where he's coming from and try to adjust to it. The same thing applies to you and your family. Both of you should learn to accept each other's families." The social worker tried to put an end to the disagreement we had against each other's families thinking that she was doing us a favor. It reminded me of kindergarten and how teachers would stop fights between kids by letting them apologize to each other. In the kids' case, it would work, but with adults, it needed more analysis to get to the root of the problem.

"I have no clue why she's that angry with my father. He had never interfered with our life," Adi pointed out a delusional fact to defend his father.

"You're not able to see what I see. He's not interfering because you're doing everything according to his standards and you're trying your best to please him," I tried to explain again.

"You're focusing on him instead of focusing on our relationship," he added.

"His influence is part of our relationship," I replied.

"Give me one example of a time that he affected us." He tried to put me in the corner.

I had millions of examples of the effect his father had on our lives, but I managed to mention only one. "Adi, for me, it's enough that he was negotiating how much I was worth when our families were discussing the amount of gold you'll have to buy to marry me. You stayed silent with your head down and with your knees shaking while your father was trying to get a lower price. He made me feel as if I was a piece of furniture."

He couldn't help but interrupt me to start the advocacy session that would justify why he was a follower, "You keep on bringing up the gold incident. You know that it's a tribal discussion that had to happen."

"Can you let me finish my point, please? You couldn't object or open your mouth in that session thinking that because it's a social event, you should follow the lead of your leader. I feel that this is what our life is based on. It's all about social conventions and what should be and shouldn't be done with the presence of your father's opinion. Adi, my case is not against your father. I am trying to explain to you that sometimes you're afraid to treat me well because you're afraid to break the image that your family has for you," I argued against his defense case.

"Saba, I am not afraid, and neither do I take into consideration what people think. If I were as you're describing, I wouldn't be sitting here trying to win you back. A lot of people I know said to me that the woman who would jail her husband shouldn't be trusted in a house, but I kept defending you. I know that what I did was wrong, and I should never raise my hand or push you or drag you. I learned my lesson. We both made mistakes, and we should both help each other fix what we broke." The philosophical character of Adi was rising to the surface. His words were comforting and scary at the same time. Giving such an example didn't feel right as if he were trying to pass me a hidden message.

My turn to be alone with Salwa came first as usual. She had a wide smile on her face when she explained, "Why don't you use Ked Al Nisa as a method with him? Men are like babies. As long as they think that they are getting what they want, they will be pleased. You can get what you want without clarifying what you want. Use manipulative actions." She clarified that the machination methods that women use are the solution to my problem.

"But, I don't know how to use the women's machination methods or know how to be malicious."

"Ked Al Nisa is not a malicious action if you use it for the benefit of your relationship. Some women get what they want without even asking," she added.

"I am not an expert in this or know how to learn it. Plus, don't you think that it's wrong to use tricks to maintain a good relationship with my husband?" I asked with an astonished reaction to her suggestions.

"Your husband is attached to the environment that he was raised in and that is understandable based on the society we live in. The fact that a Middle Eastern man is putting his ego aside to save his marriage is something that should be recognized and respected. Also, in the previous sessions, he kept on denying that he hit you, but during this session, he admitted that he did. It's quite progress, and it means that he's sincere," she elaborated to make me sympathize with Adi.

Adi's shoulders weren't spread wide open like usual after this session. He was too vulnerable and weak. He was acting like a gentleman same as he was when I first met him. He waited for me to join him in the elevator, but I tried to escape by telling him that I needed to use the bathroom. "I'll wait for you," he answered as if we were together.

It wasn't long till I met him in the street in front of the court's building.

"Can I buy you a cup of coffee?" He offered with a big smile on his face.

"I need to get back to Tahseen," I tried to escape again.

"I won't take much of your time. I know that you're sick of me repeating the same sentences, but I truly mean everything. I love you, and I want you back. Time will prove to you how much you mean to me."

"Adi, you're saying that you love me, and I am afraid that at any moment you might flip like a monster and start attacking me." I tried to explain to him that I was terrified of the Hulk that might show up any second because of the responses that he might find irritating.

"I am slowly learning to control my anger," he tried to make a promise.

"This can be achieved by seeking professional help only. You can't change without any guidance," I argued.

"Then do me a favor and give this woman a chance to help me. I know you believe that I am a good person on the inside. You fell in love with me because you saw something in me that you liked. Let's focus on this," he insisted on playing the emotions card.

"The things I liked disappeared when we got married. I was left with an irritated man who wanted his space," I responded.

"I will change because deep down I want to. I just need to feel your support and that you're there for me," he started and ended this sentence with his hand on his chest.

We both ended up on separate paths not knowing what would happen next. I was confused and uncertain, and he was hopeful. Part of me wanted to believe him, but for some reason, I couldn't.

The Provocative Wedding

Dress shopping for Yasmina's wedding was my way to escape reality for a couple of hours. I took advantage of the time that Tahseen was with his father to get some time for myself. I looked at my green eyes, pale face, and white locks of hair that newly appeared in the middle of my head through the mirror that was hanging on the wall in the fitting room. I hated the effect of my mental health that was reflected on my face and body.

I started taking pictures of different dresses to show to Layal because I wasn't capable of making any small decisions on my own. The big step of leaving Adi stole most of my energy. In the end, I was able to choose a gray/sparkly short dress. I was annoyed by the big belly bump that was making a statement through the dress. I convinced myself that if I didn't eat on that day, it wouldn't be showing through the dress as much as it was when I decided to buy it.

My father brought to my attention the fact that Yasmina's father is friends with Adi's father. "Expect to see the asshole there. Don't dare to break in front of him. Have fun and enjoy the night." Cursing Adi's father was my father's way of making me feel stronger. He would always mention the word 'son of a bitch' or 'asshole' in the middle of any sentence to make a statement.

My father was right. The asshole stepped into the wedding hall ten minutes after I was seated at the table with my coworkers. I made sure to follow my father's advice and distracted myself even though he couldn't do the same.

On that night, I danced till I couldn't feel my feet. I stayed the whole night in the circle of my coworkers not caring if I was dancing with males or females. I felt free from all the chains that I had around my neck when I was with Adi. This reminded me of the weddings that I had attended with him. He used to dance with his female friends while I couldn't dare do such with my male friends. Even when I intended to invite my male coworkers to our wedding, he made a clear statement that he didn't feel comfortable having any of them there. This led us to have a big fight because he allowed himself to invite his female friends while preventing me from doing the same. I got more furious when he kissed them on the cheeks on our wedding night. He described it as 'their way of congratulating me'. He insisted on the fact that they care about him as their brother. If the situation were reversed, he would've made a fuss out of it.

I couldn't help but notice that Adi's father was staring at the big screen that was hanging on the wall in front of him to monitor my moves and how I interacted with others around me. Adi's mother joined the dance floor for five minutes. She clapped and waved to Yasmina to congratulate her. I tried to ignore her existence, but couldn't help noticing what she was doing. In such moments, I thought of people's outfits to distract myself. I failed to distract myself this time because I remembered the horrible sense of style Adi's mother had. She was a sixty-year-old woman dressed in a sixteen-year-old girl's outfit.

The drive home was calm but suffocating because I was left alone with my thoughts for an hour. All my problems were hidden inside the loud sound of music and when I became alone, it came back to haunt me. The checkpoint lane that connects Jerusalem and Ramallah was horrible as usual. Cars were moving slowly making their way based on the instructions of the soldiers controlling the checkpoint. It was disturbing how eighteen-year-old teenagers controlled the movement of a nation between borders. These young uncarved boys and girls had the power to control, destroy, and humiliate. As a green-eyed young woman, I managed to suffer less than Palestinians with Arab features, less than a woman with a head scarf on her head, and less than anyone who doesn't have a Western appearance. Rights were distributed based on what was considered a sophisticated human. I was born with a privilege that I didn't choose.

It's hard to feel like an outsider in your own country. You're different from your own people and you don't belong to the other side. You fall into a battle that you don't want to fight. You're constantly in search of your own identity.

The Fool and the Charming Husband
~Part 4~

I tried to imagine a new life with Adi. I tried to imagine myself lost in his hands but couldn't feel safe. The idea of hugging him warmed my heart, but at the end lane of this image was a knife prepared to cut it in half.

I called Salwa to cancel our session and informed Adi about my decision via text message. Salwa refused to end everything over a phone call and demanded our actual presence. "You told me that I can end this at any time," I uttered.

"Let's discuss this in person. I need to hear your reasons. Is it something he did?" She asked with confusion.

"No, he didn't. I just don't feel that I am doing the right thing. My gut is telling me to end this. It's a dead end," I elaborated.

"I'll see you tomorrow and we'll go over everything. I won't force you to do something you're not comfortable doing. Let's just talk tomorrow," she ended the conversation.

I walked into Salwa's office with strength and determination. On the other hand, Adi walked in after me with a boiling head.

"How are you both doing?" Salwa asked.

We both answered with fine.

"Can you please explain why you want to end this?" She asked me.

"I no longer want to fight this battle," I answered.

"What about you, Adi? What do you think?" She shifted her questions to Adi.

"I think this woman doesn't need my presence in her life. She already has a job, she makes more money than I do, she goes in and out whenever she wants, she's independent…why would she need a man like me?" His answer was spiteful wanting me to be vulnerable and in need of him.

"Why don't you tell her about the shameful things that you had done during the weekend?" He pointed the question toward me.

"What did I do?" I asked.

"Don't play stupid. You come in here with tears in your eyes while you spend your time bitching around in weddings dressed like a whore. God knows how many guys you're sleeping around with," he yelled back at me.

"Watch your language, Adi," Salwa demanded.

"Don't let her fool you. She was at a wedding, dancing with ten guys, wearing a short dress that was hardly covering her ass." He stood up this time to describe how short my dress was.

"Please leave the room immediately," Salwa insisted.

"A bitch that abandoned her mother won't care about a monkey that wants her back." He moved on to shame me more.

"Adi, leave the room now," Salwa yelled back at him.

All the strength and determination that I had at the beginning disappeared and I started shaking, crying, and trying to defend myself. "It's true. I was at a wedding. But I was there with my coworkers. I used to wear the same kind of dresses when I used to go to weddings with him."

"Please take a deep breath. It's your right to go out and enjoy your time," Salwa tried to calm me down.

"I hate how vulnerable I am right now. I swear to God that I don't want to cry. He makes me weak whenever he's angry. I don't want to deal with him anymore. Please understand me," I tried to explain what she was unable to see.

"May I ask how did you even marry him? I can't understand how someone like you fell in love with someone like him." Salwa dared to wonder and question Adi's behaviors at last.

"Remember how fond you were of him and his career in the last sessions? He manages to convince strangers that he's amazing. A well-educated man who had been around the world. This is the image that he draws for others. He introduced me to the same charming personality when I first met him. This image changed when I married him. His temper controls his reactions and his behaviors," I clarified.

For the first time in four sessions, Salwa started asking me to fight this battle till the last breath, "Don't give up on any of your rights. Ask for alimony for yourself and for your child. Dress up the way you want, go out with your friends, live your life, and don't let him hold you back."

The final session ended without a closure or a final agreement. We left everything in the hands of the judge who would be handling our case. Adi refused to pay the money I asked for and I refused to make a deal with the devil without the presence of my lawyer.

When we left the building, I didn't want to walk next to him. I didn't want him to hurt me, but he managed to keep me close when he said with irritation, "I have the things that you asked for in my car. I'll get the car and meet you next to yours. Don't think that I am thrilled to walk with you toward your car."

I walked slowly behind him to achieve the goal of not walking side by side together. It was obvious that he didn't get everything out of his system when we were at Salwa's office; therefore, he kept turning his head back toward me every ten seconds to throw provocative sentences.

"You and your sisters are not that different from each other. You sure know how to enjoy your time."

"Keep an eye on your sister Layal. She leaves the house every night at two a.m. to see her boyfriends. Both of us know what that means. She waits for all of you to fall asleep and then she leaves the house. I am speaking for the sake of your reputation. Layal rides in a different car and a different man every night. Oh, how stupid of me to care for your reputation when it's already ruined. What you all did for your mother says everything about you."

I remained silent and didn't respond to anything he said until we reached my father's car. "If you leave, I'll through everything in the garbage," he threatened. I was shocked that I managed to wait for him next to the car till he came back to humiliate me again. He stopped his car in the middle of the street blocking all the cars behind him from passing by. Another car parked behind him waiting for me to leave so it could park in the parking spot that I was occupying.

Adi threw a box in the back seat of my car and stepped toward me to whisper in my ear, "You're a bitch."

This time my body disconnected itself from my mind and I reacted. I kicked him, managing to hit his bottom when he turned his back and shouted, "Kos Omak." I used the famous Arab curse word that means 'Your mother's vagina'.

Even though I reacted, Adi couldn't step out of the hysterical mood he was in. He jumped back into his car, opened the car's window, and started singing *You're a bitch* until the man behind him used the car's horn to ask him to move.

The scene of Adi driving away while singing *You're a bitch* made me lock myself in the car to protect myself.

I drove away to allow the car that was waiting to park in my place to move in. I started opening the stuff that was in the box while I was driving. I feared that he had placed suspicious items in the box. Crazy thoughts popped out of my head when I threw the certificates and the paintings that were inside the box all over the car. The box had a framed picture of me when I was a baby, a couple of portraits of myself, and certificates that I had forgotten I even had.

I sometimes think that if we hadn't been surrounded by people and cars, he would've beaten me up in the middle of the street for cursing his mother.

Oh darling, how beautiful and considerate you are in the beginning and how horrible and insensitive you are in the midst and endings.

The Mighty Elders

My brother Sami played a silent role in the whole dilemma until I was called a bitch. He gathered his friends to go and kick Adi's ass. I tried to stop him by holding on to his knees begging him not to leave the house. I followed him to the street despite the raindrops that were falling on our heads. It was a crazy rainy day that filled the neighborhood with grayness and gloominess. I felt weak at that time fearing for my brother's safety. A word is not worth his life or getting him into prison. This would've made Adi satisfied, instead of miserable.

Calling my father was the only option I had, and in return, he called the elders of our family to stop Sami. My father was the one to catch Sami and his friends before they got to Adi.

"This is what the Makhlouf family wants. They want a bloodbath and to turn the matter into a fight." Abu Husam illustrated to Sami, my father, my father's cousin, and myself. I found myself dragged into a gathering at Abu Husam's house to discuss how to avoid the Makhlouf's vicious plans.

My father's cousin stepped in to explain to Sami the current situation, showing him how weak our family was compared to the Makhlouf family. "We cannot enter a war with the Makhlouf family. Let's be honest here, we cannot even win a verbal fight against them. We fear your sister's father-in-law and we cannot defend ourselves against his sharp tongue."

I hated hearing the ringtone of my phone. Whenever I would hear the phone ringing, I would know that a disaster had happened. This time it was Abu Husam, our family's rep. He didn't ask me how I was but started with an unusual introduction. The opening of the phone call happened by cursing my father-in-law. "The dirty man called the elders of our village and told them that you hit his precious son. He asked the elders to interfere."

"But he abused me verbally first. He's the one that should be held accountable. Isn't he ashamed to say that a woman hit his son? Didn't they ask why I had to commit such an act?" I answered while holding a laugh of anger inside to try to understand what happened.

"He gathered six men from different families from our village, including one of our relatives. One of them called me to have a better understanding of what had happened. Don't worry I managed to present the full image to him, and he told me that he felt that Makhlouf's statement was fishy. I am glad that you informed me about the incident before. I managed to control the situation based on the information you passed to me yesterday. The filthy man offended our family by going to the entire village's elders except for us," Abu Husam angrily mouthed.

He moved on and mentioned the statement he presented to the man that the elders had put in charge. "I told him that it's not a fight between two families that needs interfering. It's a divorce. Two people decided to end their relationship. It's not a big national case or a public issue. The man showed his sympathy for your story and wished you all the best. I needed to put you in the picture so you know what's happening."

"I wish I was wearing heavier shoes so it would've hurt more," I said at the end of the phone call to show that I didn't regret hitting him and Abu Husam didn't argue against it.

I was able to imagine the scene of my father-in-law gathered around the elders of our village. I was sure that he was wearing one of his vintage suits that he would never change because he wouldn't spend money on new ones. He would never leave his elegant appearance fearing that his true self would be revealed. He was hiding behind the image he was able to build for himself all around East Jerusalem. He thought that people thought of him as a decent man, but the truth was that most of the men living in Jerusalem knew how deceitful and dangerous he was. The power of changing colors and manipulating the truth helped him build an army of followers. People wanted to be his friends, so he would defend them in times of despair. No one wanted to be on the other side of the table against him.

The holy city of Jerusalem was desecrated by the filthy people living in it.

One of the phrases that the men in my family kept on repeating was the sentence that my father-in-law tried to provoke them with 'A woman is controlling you?' as if I were an animal that needed to be tamed. They acted as if this question didn't affect their manhood, but I was able to sense the distress in their eyes whenever they would say it. My father-in-law knew how to stab people in their manhood, so they would act to his benefit. Thankfully, I didn't own manhood so he couldn't affect me as he would affect men in his life. In addition to that, he couldn't understand how men in my family stood behind me defending what I wanted. He thought that they'd break to his demands because they were afraid of him. Fear made them react in reverse. They wanted him out of my life so he would be out of theirs.

Feminism?

As a child, I had formed an idea about the intimacy that a woman and a man can have. It all started shaping me before I even understood what sex was. The glimpse of the images that I used to see on the TV or on the street created the image that our parents tried to postpone passing on to us.

Somehow we knew.

Somehow we were able to feel.

I kept on imagining how my life would be when I got married. I kept on living the same scene in my head over and over as I was growing older. I imagined myself wearing revealing clothes while I served the most delicious food to my husband. I think as humans we have the urge to get naked and eat. We're magnets to the pleasures of life. For me, I was able to draw that painting using the tools that others around me passed to me.

When I was young, I couldn't wear whatever I wanted because I was trained throughout my life that this body belonged to the sacred husband. Women around me convinced me that I would enjoy my body and wear whatever I wanted inside the walls of my future house when I got married. Not before marriage though. Women who wore short dresses or sleeveless shirts or didn't wear the head scarf were considered too open and too dangerous. Being free to wear what we wanted would delay or stand in the way of getting a suitable husband. I had to protect the body that belonged to my family, my husband, and society.

At some point in my life, I was vocal and defended the freedom of women over their lives. Family members and friends called me a feminist. "Your ideas are too dangerous. You will harm yourself if you stay on this path." That was the warning that one of the women around me passed to me, fearing that I would ruin myself if I became a feminist. The funny thing was that at that time I had no idea what feminism meant.

I just wanted to breathe.

I wanted to live.

My uncle once told me, "I know that our society is so fucked up and puts a lot of pressure on women when they try to free themselves and have the same benefits men have. But I don't want the change to start with my niece. Why would you be the lamb that would be slaughtered? I fear for your reputation, and I don't want it to be smudged."

He cared about my reputation fearing that it would affect his own even though we had different last names. My mother's brother didn't want me to be slaughtered but didn't mind throwing me under the bus when I dared to defend myself against the damage that my mother was causing me. In the end, he was one of the people who threw black ink at my reputation, trying to defend the acts of his sister. What mattered to him was for people to think that I was a bad daughter who rebelled against her mother rather than putting the focus on his sister's acts. I stopped being his precious niece and became my father's daughter.

Fusty Thinking

Most of the court sessions that I attended were provocative. In other words, Adi's lawyer had stupidity leaking out of his mouth. The statements he provided were from another world and were irrelevant to my case and to the twenty-first century. The top uncanny examples he presented to the judge were:

In ancient Islam, if the woman was wealthy, she would be the one responsible for paying alimony for her poor ex-husband.

She left the house without the permission of her husband and for no valid reason. In Iraq and Jordan, if a man demands his wife to stay at home and not leave the house for work and she disobeys him, the authorities would bring back the wife handcuffed to her husband.

The second example made my lawyer and the judge react and stop him. *This doesn't apply here and this example is irrelevant to where we're living.*

Saif
the Trainee

"May I ask how old are you?"

"I am twenty-seven."

"You look younger. But also too young for a divorce."

"No one likes to end a marriage unless it's hopeless."

This time this conversation occurred with the trainee lawyer who worked with my Harvey Specter lawyer.

I tried to hide my shaking hands under the table that was between us. I hated exposing my personal life to strangers. I felt that I was judged and needed to explain myself every time I would be asked about my divorce. Instead of explaining and telling stories, I learned to give brief answers.

I handed him the supporting documents that I was asked for. He went through them to see what was missing. "Where do you live now?" He stopped going through the papers and asked.

"At my father's house," I responded.

"Then we need all the bills that your father paid since you lived at his house. Water bills, electricity, and a proof of rent," he indicated.

"My father owns the house. We don't pay rent," I stated.

"Are you thinking of moving out? You know that if you rent a place on your own, then your ex-husband would pay 30% of the rent for you," he elaborated.

"I might do so, but I am not sure when," I answered with hesitation.

"Just provide us with the lease as soon as you do," he uttered.

"Can I send the documents you asked for via email, instead of coming back here?" I asked.

"We'd love to see you again, but if it's more comfortable for you, here is my card. You can find my email address and my phone number. Don't hesitate to contact me if you need anything," he politely uttered with a slight flirtation.

As always, in stressful times, I analyzed people that sit ahead of me. I couldn't help but notice that he tried to avoid eye contact. He would look at me whenever I would be staring at my phone or at the wall. I was able to sense his stares even though our eyes never crossed paths.

The white shirt he was wearing was tight enough to show his biceps. His tie was loose and his suit jacket was hanging on the back of the chair he was sitting in. I wondered how he'd look if he would have his jacket on. The image of him wearing the full suit started to shape up in my imagination. I was able to tell that he couldn't wait to get out of these formal clothes. He probably had them on him since the early morning, and I came to annoy him with my routine documents at the end of the evening. I also noticed that his beard was well groomed but his bushy eyebrows had a different statement.

The Old City of Jerusalem

The narrow alleys of the Old City of Jerusalem felt wider today. It had been a whole year since the last time I had felt the walls closing slowly, trying to trap me between its two sides. This time I felt the repaired walls that were formed of different types of rocks opening wider and wider to allow me to walk freely between them.

I started my hike from Jaffa Gate all the way to Damascus Gate. The first station that I stopped at was the tourists' market. It was the closest market to Jaffa Gate and was the cutting point between the Western Mamilla Mall and the Eastern ancient markets of Jerusalem. The tourist market that sold souvenirs lay right in the middle of the East and West.

If you start your trip to Mamilla Mall, you'll explore the European atmosphere. The modern shops distributed in an open space, the expensive pastries, expensive clothes that you hope would be on sale, and the fresh fragrances traveling out of the fancy shops through the air conditioners.

You can follow the tourists who are curious to see the bizarre and unfamiliar markets that they have heard stories about. If you put yourself in one of the tourist's shoes, you will feel that you entered Aladin's world once you step into the old Eastern market. The merchants that would be sitting on their chairs outside of their souvenir shops usually mistake me with tourists due to my Western appearance and reveal my head missing a head scarf. They would try to attract me to their shops using English, Russian, Spanish, or French. Most of them practiced several languages to communicate with foreigners. In return, I would respond in Arabic and thank them. As soon as they would know I am Arab, they would either lose interest or in some cases, they would flirt by replying back in Arabic to show that they liked the 'local product' as well.

I had some spare time till Adi would return Tahseen home. I managed to buy coffee from a young boy who was wandering around with a tray filled with cold drinks and coffee. I sat on the second stair that was facing the entrance of the Church of the Holy Sepulchre. I stared at the huge ancient building and started praying to God to protect my son and myself. I was a Muslim seeking the help of God in one of the most sacred Christian sites in the world. After all, I believed that God was everywhere.

"Saba."

I turned my head to see who was calling my name. It was Saif, the trainee lawyer that I had met at my lawyer's office.

"I was afraid that it wouldn't be you. That would've been embarrassing," he breathed.

"I'm surprised that you recognized me from behind," I replied.

"I am surprised too. I guess I wanted it to be you," he shifted to a new subject right after he breathed this sentence, "What are you doing here?"

"I am taking a break. What are you doing here?" I asked in return.

"I am crossing a path to get to Damascus Gate," he answered.

"That would be my last stop before I head back home," I emphasized.

"Do you mind if I join you? Or am I interrupting a prayer?" His request was bizarre, but I accepted it out of courtesy.

He immediately sat next to me and mouthed when we were both staring at the church and the wandering tourists. "You know, I was hesitant about which way to take and at the last minute decided to pass by this road. I am glad that I did," he said out loud.

I turned my head to look at him with confusion. He didn't turn his head back and kept staring at the entrance of the church with a smile on his face.

Saif resembled the meaning of his name by cutting everything in half. His name meant a 'sword' and, indeed, he was able to chop off any idea in half on purpose. He would throw in sentences and then shift to new topics so you wouldn't have time to respond to the risky ideas or reject his flirtation. No time was given, so no reaction would be made.

He was too spontaneous and this made me uncomfortable at first. He started a general conversation by asking me about my educational background. This subject made him open up about his educational journey. "I studied law in Jordan, came here to take the Israeli board's exams that were far more different than what I had studied in Jordan, and when I shifted to practice, it was even more different than my studies and the exams that I had here in the country."

"If you have a foxy personality, you'll make it in the world of law," I stated.

"In the world of law, I am great at changing colors. In the real world, I am simple," he uttered with a cocky tone.

"What makes you think that you can make this balance?" I asked.

"I am struggling, but managing," he answered with a smile.

I couldn't help but interrogate him: "Are you this social with all of your clients?"

"Technically, you're not officially my client. Plus, you were in my way not the other way around," he tried to tease me.

"Can we start our official social meeting with a cup of coffee whenever you're free?" He dared to spit out the invitation.

"I am sorry," I answered with a sad face that was forced out of embarrassment.

"It's just coffee," he tried to make it simple by insisting on it.

"It'll count as a date," I said.

"A date won't harm," he insisted again.

"I am still healing. It won't be fair to either of us," I tried to put an end to the request and moved on to explain myself out of courtesy. "I think that you're a brave and interesting man. I am really flattered by your offer, but I guess we crossed paths at a terrible time. Let's leave it to time."

"We'll leave it to destiny." He ended the conversation and left the stairs he was sitting at.

As he walked away, he stopped and turned himself toward me calling me by my name, "Saba. We will meet again."

"We will for sure," I replied with a smile.

Massive Destruction

I was a well-respected woman in the outer world versus an unappreciated woman in the inner walls of my conflicted relationship. A two-sided mirror that reflected two realities. A tiny crack was expanding between the two reflections. Adi caused the crack and was the reason behind its expansion. His fingers were shifting slowly, pressing on the mirror trying to break it. His hand was bleeding, but he didn't care. He hurt himself before he was able to completely break me.

I was running in circles between the tribes that were formed of all sorts of men. I was introduced to educated men, powerful men, menial men, weak men, and sick men. The next destination that Adi led me to was the men inside the institution where I worked.

Adi dared to try to ruin my career as a teacher.

"Can you please follow me?" The principal of the school whispered when he leaned toward the table where I was sitting. I folded the paper that I had in my hand and slid it into one of my books that were left out on the table.

"Is something wrong?" I whispered back.

"Just follow me," he commanded. I did as he asked and followed him to his office.

"Close the door behind you," he commanded again.

I walked slowly till I reached the chair that was facing the principal. He didn't sit behind his desk. He chose to sit across from me. He grabbed a piece of paper that was lying on his desk and looked back at me. He breathed in and out before he spoke about the printed email that was in his hand. "I don't believe that I should interfere or ask about your personal life. But this email is forcing me to. I am sorry if I'll make you uncomfortable." He stopped and breathed in and out again before he continued explaining what was in the email. "Adi sent me an official email accusing you of being a selfish mother and describing you as a bad role model. He's claiming that you're a threat to your students." He stopped again when he noticed the tears that were splashing out of my eyes.

"Why are you crying?" He asked.

"This man surely knows how to find ways to ruin my life," I answered with a shaky voice.

"I am not here to judge you or accuse you of anything. You need to know that we're here for you," he tried to assure me that this email would not affect my job.

I was furious and filled with anger. I stood in a classroom filled with students while staring at my hands, imagining myself holding Adi's camera in my hands. I let go of the camera, waiting for it to smash and break into pieces. I wanted to break what he valued the most. In reality, I broke my own mug that I got from my students.

The best influencer in the world! We love and appreciate you <3. The words that were written on the mug by my students faded away.

My husband attacked my image and the career that I had started building for myself. Five students rushed to help me clean the shattered glass that was all over the classroom.

My beloved husband followed me to the place where I felt honored and appreciated. I knew that he was poisonous, but I didn't expect him to get that low and attack my source of income. He thought that if I lost my job and suffered financially, I would run back to him to take me back.

Rise from the ashes like a phoenix.
Surprise everyone around you.
Whenever someone tries to burn you, kill them with the light coming out of you.
Their matches are your cane that will help you get to your destination.
Whenever they think that they ruined you, show them how you will shed your skin like a snake.
The labor of your rebirth will hurt, but it'll bring a new blessing into your life.

A Clean Chapter

Uncertainty is always hard and painful. You feel lost and you drown in your thoughts waiting for a savior.

If you're lost in your own bubble, you won't see that you're the solution. Once you take two steps back and look at your life from a distance, you will realize what's best for you.

You should never surrender when you're inside the hole. Wait till you're outside and then decide.

You feel that the nightmare will last forever.

You keep trying to get to the end of the tunnel with no success. As if it's getting darker and longer.

You pause for a while trying to understand the maze you are stuck at.

You even consider going backward to the road you know instead of going forward. You force yourself to resist and run forward again.

During the process of healing, I learned to live with my own self before allowing outsiders to get closer to me. The equation of putting two people together can never work out if one of them is broken.

I managed to spend some time cleansing my circle before letting anyone fall into it. I knew that I wasn't everyone's type, but similar characters managed to find each other. We attract what we think we deserve. Your magnet will help you find your way and your people.

I grew up with a narcissistic mother that made me think that being abused is normal. She helped others drag me down because she thought that I should live the same life she had. Adi's sister had the same character. These two women were helping pass on the abuse they had experienced. They knew no other truth. They never felt what it would be like to be loved. Women were sewing the continuation of traditions to help the man. They served the purpose of satisfying men around them.

This applied to Adi's presence in my life as well. I attracted him into my life because being abused was the only thing I had ever experienced. Adi and my mother were the only form of home I ever had.

Anger was all I was able to feel whenever I spoke about my mother. I kept on blaming her instead of forgiving her. The effect she had on my life was strong and did not allow me to think about forgiveness.

I look at her now with pity. I just feel bad for her. It sounds horrible, but how can someone control her own feelings? Eventually, I learned to let go of the hate I had felt for so long. I allowed her back into my life while maintaining a distance. I stopped ignoring her texts and calls. I gave short answers whenever we spoke, but it counted.

I never admitted to her that I forgave her. Yet my presence in her life was satisfying enough for both of us.

When I look back at the journey I went through, I praise myself for leaving the miserable life that I would've been trapped in if I hadn't fought back. I managed to win despite all the stones that I had to walk over, the stressful court sessions, the people who tried to manipulate me, and even my own negative thoughts. My society tried to convince me that divorce is bad for women. They say that women should be patient and accept their destiny even if it means staying in an abusive relationship. I was about to believe this myth until I experienced it. I appreciated my freedom when I regained it. My life began and my options expanded when I learned to say 'No' with an open chest.

As Sweet As Kunafeh
Saif

You never think that the pain will ever disappear while you are in the middle of the storm. Two years have passed since my separation. The endless court sessions, the unreasonable arguments, the lawyers, and my ex officially became in my past tense.

After the divorce, the fire in Adi's chest cooled down. We stopped fighting, and we started communicating as two strangers who were bound by an arrangement. Our son was our connecting point.

Tahseen's visits to his father's house became more stable. The free hours that I had to myself helped me get out and socialize more. I returned to my true self. The human inside me came back to life. Time healed the cracks that I thought would stay open.

I prepared my son for his weekly visit to see his father on a Sunday afternoon. The weather outside was hot and dry. I started debating whether to take a long nap till he would return home or go out. I was hesitant till the house became empty. After all, Tahseen was adding a special flavor to our new home. Not having him around made it feel soulless.

I forced myself out and somehow found myself walking toward the church of the Holy Sepulcher. I bought a cup of Arabic coffee and sat on one of the stairs facing the massive entrance of the church. The huge square was almost empty. Usually, it would be filled with tourists, but COVID happened and messed up our normal.

I took out my headphones and played a happy song. I learned to avoid sad songs to stay in a cheerful mood.

I felt a hand touching my shoulder, interrupting my thoughts and music. I removed one of my headphones and looked at the hand that had touched my shoulder.

"I am sorry if I scared you. I kept on calling your name till I realized that you had headphones on," words came out of Saif's mouth.

I didn't know what to answer, but it felt like it hadn't been long since we met at the same place, even though two years had passed.

"I was about to prepare my fist to attack," I blundered.

He stepped in front of me, forcing me to look up toward him.

"I see you're having coffee. I can't ask you out for coffee this way," he charmingly said.

"You can buy me kunafeh. I know a good place nearby," I boldly offered.

"Wow. We're making progress. What happened to you? Are you the same person I met years ago?" He jokingly asked.

"You're talking, as if you knew me before," I uttered.

"You rejected me before, and now you want to have kunafeh with me. You just made my year." He couldn't hide the big smile that was on his face.

"Your year? Not even your day?" I asked with confusion while still looking up with my hand over my head because of the sun.

"I'll tell you what I mean when we start eating the kunafeh." He moved two steps to the side to offer me some shade then asked me to guide him toward the kunafeh shop.

I walked by his side in the middle of the market of the Old City till we made it to the sweets shop. The shop was filled with all kinds of traditional sweets. Kunafeh and baklava were my favorites.

He guided the way when we entered the shop even though I was the one who had recommended the place. He took the lead and ordered two plates of kunafeh.

We sat facing each other with an awkward smile on our faces. We just stared at each other for a minute before he mouthed. "After you stopped visiting our office, I found myself taking the same route whenever I had a chance, hoping to run into you. A whole year passed since the last time I saw you. This is why I told you that you made my year."

I blushed without realizing that my face turned red.

I zoomed out for seconds and mumbled in my head, "Saba, you deserve a life that is as sweet as this kunafeh."